# The Breach House Anthology

## Volume II

# The Breach House Anthology

## Volume II

*An Anthology of Prose and Poetry by Members of*
*The Breach House Writers' Group*

Edited by Edward Lemond

Breachhousebooks
Barachois, New Brunswick

Front and Back Cover Concept
Roméo Savoie

Lemond, Edward

The Breach House Anthology Volume II

ISBN: 978-0-9780510-8-2

First paperback edition 2012

Breachhousebooks
Chemin de la Brèche
Barachois, N.B.

# Contents

*Black and White Series # 5, Nancy King Schofield, 2012*

# Foreword

In the spring of 1999 four people who loved to write drove from Moncton, N.B. to my artist's studio on the Breach Road in Grand Barachois. I invited these friends to discuss the idea of forming a writers' group. Because writing is a solitary pursuit that improves with positive feedback and critique, we decided to meet one day each month for the purpose of motivating each other and creating an audience for our written work. When I suggested we choose a name for the group, one of us said that she had always wanted to belong to a gang. After a short discussion we quickly agreed to become the Breach House Gang.

The process we began that day and the friendship nurtured over thirteen years becomes stronger, as does the quality of our writing. All of our members have been published and many have received special recognition, grants and awards. Our first anthology, in 2010, was well received not only by friends and family but also by the broader public, made evident by a successful book launch at La Teraz Gallery in Moncton. Since that time we had to say farewell to Anne Levesque when she was relocated to Nova Scotia but David Skyrie and Zev Bagel have since joined the Gang, bringing our total number to ten. Each of these writers brings a wealth of knowledge, life experience, and a unique style of writing with him. Our Sunday afternoon meetings are informative, constructive and accompanied by a feeling of camaraderie.

Several months ago we decided with enthusiasm to embark on our second anthology. When I sat to write the introduction, I thought about how the writing forms move freely from writer to writer, unrestricted by expectations or dictates. We listen closely, we give support where we can, and we do not hesitate to offer criticism where it will help strengthen the writing. I hope that you, the reader, will find examples of strong writing in these pages, writing that invites you in and will not let you go.

Nancy King Schofield
Chemin de la Brèche
Grand Barachois, New Brunswick

*Beauty and Strength, Elaine Amyot, 2012*

# Elaine Amyot

## Obsession

On a Friday, as she was leaving, my friend Elizabeth made me promise to write a paragraph – something new. Forget the memoir for a while. About obsession? I said. Why, oh why did I choose that particular subject? It was really the subject that chose me, for the word was out of my mouth before I had time to think about it. No time to cogitate. I should have chosen 'shoes' or 'ships' or 'sealing wax,' but some devil in me came out with OBSESSION.

The idea of writing that paragraph became a torment. Rather than begin to write I compulsively ate an excessive amount of candied nuts – nuts given to my husband for his birthday the day before. Not being satisfied with that, I read a Gail Bowen thriller until well past midnight. I was consumed with the urge to find out *why* the murderer had killed. I knew *who* he was and could have gone to bed in peace but I was obsessed with the notion of reading the novel to its end despite fatigue and sore eyes.

I went to bed but not to sleep. The thought of writing that paragraph became an *idée fixe*. Visions of past obsessions surfaced without my willing. There were many. Some, in retrospect, were amusing, some painful, others humiliating. They appeared relentlessly until daylight came.

I remembered the intense feeling of being out of control. There was a motor in me that had lost its governor. It was in charge. There was a feeling of danger, rather exciting because I didn't know what would happen next. I was no longer able to decide what to do. I was aware that what I did was harmful (to me), but I had to do it nevertheless.

These obsessive behaviours were shielding me, they protected me from a reality I was not ready to face. In eventually facing them I became free – until the next fanatical obsession took over.

## Mildred

**I** remember. I remember Mildred. We pronounced it Mill/Drude. We being the people who lived on St. Thomas Street, Joliette, Quebec, in the thirties and early forties.

She was a year older than I and was much admired because she was …. Blonde. My dark hair and eyes were ordinary and common, and I considered myself plain.

We both had long ringlets, but her hair, not being naturally curly like mine, had to be put up at night, in rags. Mother's face would register disdain when she saw these thin blond curls. She was proud of my thick hair and felt superior because to do my hair, no rags were needed.

The morning ritual of ringlet making was long and painful. Each strand had to be combed to get rid of snarls, then it was dampened and wound around her index finger and released to let dry. The ringlets would fall in a hair-do common at the time – a style made popular by the Dionne Quintuplets. Their images were seen in so many places – they were more popular than the Royal family.

To get back to Mildred. She was born with a deformed left hand that she kept hidden in the folds of her dress. (We wore dresses then, never trousers.) Perhaps it was the need for secrecy – a need to hide, to cover up that made her so devious. She had a bright smile but there was something not quite honest or clear in her expression. It seemed to conceal an uncertainty, a wish to present what is expected, not a genuine feeling.

She lived next door to us, in an upstairs apartment, with her parents Gertie and Arthur Vincent (pronounced en français). I remember the kitchen best of all. It seemed forever sunny. It was *so clean.* The linoleum, a pale green and cream – colours popular in the thirties – was so glossy, having been scrubbed and mopped weekly or daily, I could see myself. There were no plants, no books, no magazines, no baskets holding mendings or knittings like there were in my house. On the kitchen table, I remember, near the chair Arthur sat in, was an ornament – an enormous green ceramic frog, its mouth open to receive Arthur's cigarette butts.

Arthur worked at the local saw mill (called "Copping's"), and he would arrive home covered with sawdust. He would take off his overalls in the shed. All houses had sheds – it's where, in these "hangars" as they were called, the firewood was kept. After shedding his overalls Arthur would come into the kitchen to sit in his chair. I don't recall ever seeing him anywhere else in the apartment. The kitchen was the only place he was permitted to smoke. He would sit there for a long time. Sometimes, without warning, he would keel over and fall on the floor. I don't remember anyone thinking this was unusual, or helping him up. I guess he did more in the shed than take off his overalls.

The apartment had a front room – un salon. We never ventured into this room but looked in as if it were a 'vitrine' (a store-front window) in Eaton's Department Store in Montreal. The blind was kept down so my memory of it is of a brownish gloomy place where a sofa and two chairs of a dark plush material never were moved. There was a fascinating ashtray on a pedestal of copper-coloured metal with a box-like structure for matches and cups for holding cigarettes. It was never used. When the family moved a few years later, we saw this furniture, unused and brand-new looking, pass before our eyes, into a van.

The entrance to her apartment was a steep stairway leading to a dark hallway lit up by a suspended lampshade which had chunks of coloured glass – emerald greens, deep blues, vivid reds and warm golds. I was always spellbound by these colours. One day Mildred suggested that we throw my metal doll carriage down the stairs. Whatever she suggested I agreed to – that's how I was. We threw the doll carriage several times and enjoyed the clamour and the satisfaction that we were breaking rules. My mother could not understand why we had done this. Neither could I, at the time.

Mildred's room was small and very neat. She covered one wall with clippings of our favourite movie stars. We thought Hedy Lamarr the most beautiful and Deanna Durbin the most talented. When Mildred saw my brother's room, her eyes were wide with shock. His bed was a playground – a landscape strewn with books, small stuffed bears, trucks, cannons, plasticene soldiers ready for battle or shot dead with BBs, and a favourite dark-red rabbit called Pin Pin (pronounced en français) that wore an embroidered blouse and teal-coloured vest.

M. et Mme. Vincent were an unusual couple on our street. They never went to church or to Mass. Many people went to Mass daily and certainly on Sunday. Arthur kept chickens in a small hut, surrounded by chicken wire. He also kept a pet turtle. He claimed a snapping turtle had bitten off part of his left hand index finger. He said he'd saved that tip and to prove it would show us a match box that had cotton batting in it – with the tip of the finger. We were so innocent we didn't realize the box had a hole in it.

Arthur was a great storyteller. We loved to hear him telling us of strange events. One of these was about a trip by car to Berthierville on a foggy night. He and Gertie gave a man a ride. They claim he was Jesus Christ. They were very sure of this.

Mildred knew I was very unhappy in Grade One. I did not have a leather book bag like everyone else, and for this I stood out as different (of course I was that already, being French). My mother had bought me a neat little dark blue cardboard valise that I hated. Mildred had a solution to my problem. Why not place the hated valise in the hole of the basement of the building next to the school? This was the blacksmith's shop, which we knew to be the case because of the small copper anvil embedded in the sidewalk. We placed the valise out of sight, under the flooring of the shop. When I got home I told my mother I had lost it. She said nothing. Did she know I was lying? I've always thought so. But she said nothing. Instead, she got me the coveted leather bag, which lasted until high school.

Mildred ventured to do things I would never have done on my own. On the way home one afternoon we stopped in front of a small house. On this street were several small houses, with no porch, no lawn, but opening on to the sidewalk. The door was open in one of them and we saw a coffin inside the room. In it was a pale-faced woman. There were candles about, and a very hushed atmosphere. Mildred was not deterred. She went in and looked at the corpse. Of course I followed. I could not recall ever having seen a dead person, forgetting that when I was 2 ½ I'd seen my Grandfather Brunet in his coffin.

In Joliette at this time lived a Mademoiselle Lavallée, She taught piano and organized a "Cercle des Petits". We were taught to dance, to sing, to recite and to play act. Once a year "Le Cercle" held a concert in the Collège Classique theatre. This was a professional theatre – lots of ornamentation, good lighting and a very interesting collection of props backstage. Most of the gowns were 18th Century – red satins, green silks, lavender chiffon, pale yellow taffetas.

One year Mildred was the star. She was Sleeping Beauty in "La belle au bois dormant". She was beautiful with her golden curls and her long lavender dress. When the Prince sat her up (there was no kissing!) her hair ribbon – the same colour as the dress – fell to the floor. She said this embarrassed her but I thought it was natural – lovely.

My five-year-old brother became a star also. He wore a child's version of a Royal Air Force uniform. He doesn't remember this for I think he was petrified. He was there alone on the huge stage, reciting a poem whose title was "Je suis un homme". He had a lisp which made his performance all the more memorable – but not to him.

When Mildred left it was my turn to be a star. I had an 18$^{th}$ Century dress of pale yellow taffeta – with flounces and panniers and a headdress like those worn by Kate and previous Royal women, called "fascination". I danced the minuet from Don Giovanni. I was frightened but did as I was taught. The Bishop commented on my gracefulness. He also commented on my being Protestant.

The Vincent family moved. My mother was relieved for I would get into scrapes following Mildred who usually managed to have me take the blame. Did I become more certain of myself – less prone to be a follower? Not until some years went by.

I last heard from her when I was at St. John's Hall in Quebec City. Her letter was full of grand news – that she was engaged to the son of the mayor of Westmount. I wrote back that I was dating a tennis player from Mexico. So ended our contacts.

I am still ashamed of having written that letter. I don't like to admit that I too can be dishonest and devious.

# Eclipse

**H**is name was Alberto. When I first pronounced it, placing the accent on the last syllable, as we do in French, he corrected me. "C'est Alberto!" He was Italian.

The war had been over for two years, and he and his sister Maria had just arrived from Italy to be with their Grandmother Nicoletti. They did not talk of the war. Life on the farm in Base-de-Roc, a farm only a little farther down the road from Tante Lily's where my family lived at the time, must have been a very different experience.

It was summer. I was on holiday from boarding school, glad to be home. Base-de-Roc was new to me. I knew none of our neighbours, but an opportunity to know them came when our barn cat had four kittens. We already had three cats so homes had to be found for the kitts. I bicycled down 'le rang Base-de-Roc,' met and chatted with the farmers' wives, found homes for the cats and was delighted to meet Maria and Alberto.

He was foreign looking, exotic, with full lips, grey eyes and skin the colour of olives. Olives that I had first tasted recently in Tante Alice's kitchen. Olives that were, to me, unusually strange, so smooth with their out-of-the-ordinary taste, mysterious with their stuffing of something a surprising red.

I remember him as always being astride his bicycle. When he stopped to talk he would take a cigarette out of a pack that he kept in his shirt pocket, insert it in an ivory-coloured holder, hold this against his chest, and, to emphasize a point, would gesture with it elegantly. I thought this a striking pose, fascinating as I did his accent, so different from that of the local boys.

My young brother was not impressed with Alberto. He considered him affected – a fake, a fraud. Words were not strong enough to show his contempt; therefore, when Alberto rode by on his bicycle, my brother would make loud, extravagant, exaggerated retching noises.

That year, during the Thanksgiving holiday, Alberto and I occasionally bicycled together. One evening we found ourselves on an unknown road – deserted, no cars, no houses, no nearby trees. It was quiet, no bird song, only the large, huge sky. It was my favourite time of day – 'entre chien et loup.' The sun had set but the night had not yet come. The sky was a transparent glass-like blue green. It was a magical

16

moment, a feeling of being suspended in time. The sun had left us, the unknown was about to present itself.

We stopped and were still astride our bicycles. Without a word we looked at a huge full October moon. As we looked, a red shadow appeared in it, and as we gazed, spellbound, the moon became a deep red. We turned toward each other and very softly, tentatively, tenderly, our lips touched. We were filled with awe, lost for words and not wanting to break this spell of wonderment. We silently left that moment of enchantment.

## The Sack

It began with a flash view of a man holding the hand of a very pregnant woman. In his other hand, a large, full, green garbage bag.

I saw them for an instant before they vanished from sight between buildings.

The year was 1992; the day, June 30th; the time, 17h30; the place, the northwest corner of Highfield and St. George Streets, in Moncton.

That split second image was like a stop action photograph.

"Was that P. with the pregnant woman?" I asked the friend I was driving home.

"Yes, he's got someone to think about now besides himself," she replied.

That scene was etched in my brain. It kept recurring, unbidden and with such force that I could feel the impact physically, in my gut. I felt there was a powerful engine in charge, going at full speed, and it had lost its governor. It would not stop. I was unable to sleep. Food no longer interested me. This condition, of being driven by an unknown force, was so intense that I sought the help of a psychiatrist friend.

At the end of our first session the psychiatrist friend asked me to draw what was in the garbage bag. The sack. The idea stunned me, for I had never dared open up the sacks that appeared in my art or in my dreams. But since this one wasn't mine (or so I thought at the time), I was able to take courage and look.

Twenty charcoal drawings were the result.

Sacks had begun to appear in my dreams when I was ten. I had a recurring dream of a man coming into my room silently; he never spoke but before I could open my eyes he would slip a sack over my head, which he then tied around my throat with a rope. Holding this, he would lead me off the bed, into the living room, out of the house, and throughout the town. In the morning I would wake up tired but relieved to be able to breathe freely once more.

## My Future Husband's Ex

**I** thought the obsession of 1992 would be the last. Not so. A year later, in November, 1993, another one began. This one crept up on me.

It was evening. E. and I were in his newly opened bookstore – his first in Moncton. I was translating into French a poem he'd written about his father.

The phone rang. When he answered, his voice was low, warm, intimate. He said he'd call back in half an hour. Then he told me the call was from a woman he knew, that she lived in New York City, and that he was no longer in an intimate relationship with her.

It didn't sound like a definite break so I asked him to please make up his mind – to sever that relationship before beginning one with me.

The next day he told me he'd done that. He didn't talk about her, which made me very curious to know more. I wanted to know what she looked like, what she wore, did she like opera. I wanted to know, but didn't ask, if they'd known each other a long time, where had they met, and why they were no longer together.

I fell into the machinery of OBSESSION.

In the bookstore was a back room filled with many boxes – not one of them securely closed. Of course this meant that when I had the opportunity I would look into them – knowing it was snooping, and that it was none of my business. Doing this in secret, on the sly, was exciting – I would feverishly look to find photographs showing a tall attractive woman wearing, in one photo, a print dress, princess style, square necked – a little girl look popular in the 80s. There were other framed photographs, of her in front of a fire at a beach and many unframed ones, of her in a bathing suit. She had – oh agony – a beautiful slender body.

I continued furtively looking into the boxes. Part of the obsession was the need to do this secretly, to do it in a state of mind that was abnormal, insane. My picture of myself, as an honest, outspoken sort of person, was being put to the test. Here I was engaging in something I knew to be base, devious. There were so many boxes, and I would not rest until I had gone through them all.

Eventually, I did go through them all. Somewhere along the line E. discovered what I was doing and recognized it for the obsession it was – one that hurt him as well as me. He decided to put all the contents of the boxes into large green garbage bags to be collected by the city garbage collections. He did not include a beautiful dark green corduroy quilt, lined with rabbit fur – it was too precious. Eventually we gave the quilt to an artist friend who uses fur in her work.

The garbage bags sat in front of our house, waiting to be picked up. At 3 o'clock in the morning I put on a dressing gown and slippers, took a small flashlight and went outside – to take inventory.

I have a vivid recollection of the contents. Here is the list.

Two flannel bed sheets, dark green

Two large bath towels, jade green

One green plaid shirt, a dark green winter jacket, winter boots

A mauve acrylic nightgown

A cotton dress, white with large yellow stripes, badly mended

Pantyhose – I didn't count – but many

Socks white, running shoes, fleece-lined slippers

Several blue jeans

One pair delicate pink silk panties

One pair pink cotton ones – with a blood stain on them

Flesh coloured lace trimmed bras – medium size

A sophisticated looking black silk zippered bag holding

Mascara, Q-tips, bandaids, a bottle of lense cleaner

Two white T shirts – one with a border of lace

Three very large T shirts – one with a tiger on the front

Another with a wolf or dog

A third with a logo of a NY state new age resort

A very long T shirt in a deep blue green –

A colour she used in the room she had at the Lunenburg Attic Owl

A colour that is said to be a favourite of divorced women.

No longer having objects to find I turned to reading E.'s journals. Oh, not the entries he wrote while with me but the ones written when he was with her. It was despicable, insane – but I couldn't help myself. I did leave notes, saying, I've read those pages. As if that would somehow make it more acceptable.

The presence of this unknown-to-me woman went with me everywhere. She seemed to be in the car, when we went to Halifax, to Lunenburg, to places along the Eastern seaboard – to all of the places I knew the two of them to have visited.

I was so troubled I asked my nun friend what to do. "You have a cross to bear," was her answer. I took that to mean that I needed to accept this madness and pray to have it go away.

It coloured my emotional life with darkness. When E. told me that he felt this obsession to be threatening our well being I immediately felt sane again. I couldn't face losing him. So the darkness left, to return only seldom.

Walking along our tidal river, observing the pheasants that come to our back garden, looking at the night skies, working in my studio, talking to friends, family – these activities kept the obsession in the background.

For a long time it was there, then it stopped.

I don't understand why they happen – the obsessions. Do I need to concentrate on something forbidden, secret, instead of facing a reality that I find threatening? It is a mystery to live with. I recall Keats and his concept of "negative capability" – to be capable of being in "uncertainties, mysteries, doubts, without any irritable reaching after fact and reason."

I live with that.

*Black and White Series # 6, Nancy King Schofield, 2012*

# Zev Bagel

## Bender's Box
## Excerpts

### 7

**D**addy Bender's hand wraps itself right around mine. It's enormous and warm and comfortable and rough and rather hairy. It holds me not so tightly that it restrains me but just to show that we are companions.

We're on the Common. The two of us. We know the Common very well. Out of our door, past Aunty Sally's and Jacky's, over the cattle-grid and here we are. The other way, down Park Street to the big busy road, across to the nursery school and beyond is frightening and unknown. Here I'm grown-up and safe with Daddy Bender by my side. He knows everything and fears nothing.

We tramp across the vast expanse of grassland, trudging up the hills, dashing across into the dips until home is distant and out of sight.

"Look, there's our favourite place."

There in the direction of his pointing finger, I can see the great fallen-down tree trunk that we have discovered. I let go of his hand and run. The first bit leaves me gasping as I rush down into the dip and my legs judder up into my body; the second bit, up the gentle slope is easier but by the time I reach the tree trunk I'm breathless and it's hard to clamber up its side.

Reach up, foot on this lump sticking out, hold on to this other one, body hugging the rough edges on the trunk; extract this arm trapped underneath me, haul myself over and I'm on the top. Just time to dangle my legs over the side as Daddy Bender catches me up, puffing out his cheeks, blowing out whistles of air. He lowers himself down onto the trunk and sits beside me, his feet firmly on the grass.

We sit here panting. His hand goes into his jacket pocket. What will it pull out this time? It's a small brown object looking like a tiny, pointed egg.

"See what I picked up. It's an acorn. Do you know that if we plant this acorn it will grow into a big oak tree like that one over there? We're sitting on an old oak tree that has died and fallen over, so this tree trunk was once a tiny acorn like this."

The thing in the palm of his hand would turn into this tree trunk! I pick up the acorn while Daddy Bender talks on. I examine it between my fingers, squeeze it, turn it, stroke it, and try to make it become a tree.  He's talking about London now, as he often does.

"What's London?"

"It's a big town."

"What's a town?"

"Well, Hungerford is in the country and we came here because of the war.  In the country we have the Common, with cows and sheep and the farm and the river and lots of trees and open space.  A town is full of roads and houses and shops and cars and is much more crowded with people."

Somewhere inside my head I can see a picture; no, two pictures.  One is quite clear, from my book.  Lambs frolic about, a little girl wearing a long flowing dress; a border of flowers surrounds it all.  This is the country.  The town is harder to capture, the picture is not from a book; it's hazy and colourless and keeps fading.  There is a wide road, cars, tiny people hurrying along; what seems like smoke.  But I can't tell where the country ends and the town begins.  I think it has something to do with the flowery border, because when I see the picture in my head, the lambs try to leap over the flowers into the grey smoke.

Daddy Bender is still talking.

"After the war we shall go back to London and you'll see what a town is."

"What's the war?"

Daddy Bender talks on but I can't get any pictures and it's boring, until he produces a coin from one of his secret pockets and shows me the King.  Another pocket; his watch on a chain pressed close to my ear so I can hear its ticking.  Back it goes.  This time, between his fingers, a small white ball.  I reach out; it disappears.  It's not in this hand, but that one.  He pops it out of his ear, bounces it on the tree trunk, catches it, bounces it and it sails away.  I run to pick it up and we play with the ping-pong ball until, quite mysteriously, it gets lost and neither of us can find it.

"We shall have to go back."

We set off, exploring bushes on the way down to the fence where we wait until the train puffs its way along in the distance.

Back up the slope we have to go near the cows, but Daddy Bender's legs hide me from them.  Along the path, smoke rising from the cottages.  Legs feel heavy.  Daddy Bender won't carry me, holds my hand tightly as we step gingerly across the cattle-grid.

The kitchen is warm and steamy and full of conversation and cooking.

8

Now there was a man.  Most of what I know about him; where he came from and the things he did and was known for, comes from the stories about him that my aunt would have told me.  But to me, my great-grandfather wasn't anything to do with his background and his courage and compassion for other people.  It was all to do with the love he gave me.

He was my hero.  There's no doubt about that.  The thing is; I know the impact was that I always tried to be like him.  Now is that nurture or isn't it?  Or, come to think of it, is it genetic?  Don't really know the answer to that.  Probably doesn't matter.

What does matter, to me anyway, is the direct link between us. I can't figure out how, but I know that no matter what I do, I'm who I am at least partly because of Daddy Bender.  And of course my mother. And my grandmother.  Three generations of Benders all moulding me before I was ten.  Did they have any idea, or were they just being who they were?

9

Spluttering, flickering, yellow, blue, jumping, dancing, hissing, cracking, showering red sparks, billowing white-and-grey-and-black smoke from deep inside its throat to puff it upwards into the dark cavernous chimney.

Mummy had just made this fire; I saw her roll up the newspapers tightly, screwing them round into knots, humming over the sound of the crunching paper.  She'd knelt down and leant forward, a strand of her dark hair as usual slipping out from underneath her headscarf and falling over her forehead.  I watched with my hand on her back as she placed the paper rolls on top of the grate.

"Fetch the sticks for me."

I'd picked up some of the wood that Daddy Bender had chopped up yesterday and had deposited in a neat bundle at the side of the hearth; handed it to her.  She peered into the coal-bucket.

"Oh dear, it's nearly all gone."

She delved into the bucket and picked out some small pieces of coke and a few chunks of coal, putting them on top of the pile of paper and wood.  She flicked back her strand of hair, giving a little click of

25

her tongue and turned to me. A peculiar black mark had appeared across her forehead. I pointed at it to show her. She put her finger on her nose, leaving another black smudge on the end of it and pulled a face at me, making me laugh.

"Now for you."

Her finger poked at my nose; my heart jumped, a squeal leapt out of me, I turned around to hide in the kitchen before she could catch me. But she didn't follow.

When I went back she was kneeling at the hearth again, a box of matches in her hand. I watched from a little distance as she selected a match and struck it against the side of the box. A flame burst into life. She held the match downwards until the flame softened and curled, then held it against an edge of paper. The paper darkened, twisted, lit up; the flame crept, grew and began to play against the sticks.

Mummy turned, but she was no longer threatening to blacken my nose. Instead she picked up the wire guard that always stood flat against the wall, and concentrating on her job, fixed the sides together so that it became a cage. She stood it in front of the fire, picked up the empty coal-bucket and went outside.

I can see right inside your belly; into your moving, changing, magic soul. What are you, licking the sticks with your yellow tongues, spitting playfully at me, whispering secret messages? What are you trying to tell me?

The guard keeps you from me; how can I understand you with this barrier between us? Kneeling down with my face close to the mesh means I can see better, except for this one black wire in the way. The mesh moves easily so I can pry it apart to make a good gap for my eyes to view unhindered.

Flames leap higher, small black particles float gently upwards, a deep soft roaring beckons.

Fist just squeezes through the gap; arm follows but sticks at elbow; pull at wire a bit more with free hand; push elbow until, with a lurch, it slips through; wriggle closer to the guard; shoulder touches wire; now thumb can reach your red heart.

Scream! Scream a high, loud, long, piercing, unending, pain-pitched scream. Scream the agony, scream the horror, scream the treachery. Scream at the flames holding fast to my thumb, scream at my helplessness, scream at the searing obscenity of melting flesh. Scream until my body fills up with the sound and turns into a blackness inside my head.

Scream for Mummy.

Distant footsteps hurrying; a crash and clatter; Mummy's voice crying out to me, Mummy framed in the doorway, her mouth open, her eyes seeking me; beside me; pulling me back; freeing me. The thumb is a blackened and smoking stick. A sweet, sickly and somehow familiar smell rises from it.

For weeks the Thumb is the centre of everyone's attention. The doctor has encased it in bandages and pulled over it a black leather fingerstall tied with thongs around my wrist. The days are filled with regular viewings, coverings with Vaseline, changes of bandages. Things happen to it; the nail curls back, goes soft, falls off. The Thumb begins to return to its pink colour, a new nail begins to emerge. But its shape is strange. The whole thumb is different, rough and stubby at the end, shorter and fatter than the other one.

It's my right thumb. Now, by only glancing at it, I can tell which is my right hand and even my right foot. Grandma thinks I'm very clever for two-and-a-half.

## 10

Wide light blue eyes gaze steadily down into mine. Unblinking, they seem to pierce through me, work their way into my head. I look deep into them to see what I can find. I find warmth, trust, friendship. Max has eyes that never blink, a mouth always open in a little 'o' making him look in a state of constant surprise. Freckles play around his face, almost obliterating his stubby nose. His hair is a straw-covered cascade straggling down his forehead.

Mummy is with Auntie Sally and Jacky in the kitchen. Jacky is too small to come and play with Max and me; in any case we have secret things to do.

After our long gaze into each other's eyes, Max grabs my hand and we go round the back into the yard.

What is it to be? Lying in the short stubbly grass or hiding in the long wavy weeds? Bouncing a ball on the concrete slabs or dragging feet on the gravelly patches? Climbing some of the small trees or poking around under the untidy shrubs? Playing hide-and-seek in the wooden lavatory cubicles and cement coal-sheds or running up the small hillock with the door in it that goes down into the air-raid shelter? Or peering down the well?

Whatever we do, we always spend some time with the well. Max likes it best when we lie on our tummies and call our names down into the depths, hearing them reverberate, sounding hollow and distant, bouncing our laughter around inside the earth. Dropping stones is good too; down they go out of sight, and if we hold our breath and lie with our ears over the side of the well we can hear the delicate plop as they reach the secret at the bottom.

Max decides we should go to the well and turn the handle. We have to move stealthily, parting the low bushes surrounding the well, making sure no one is watching. It needs both of us to hold the rusting handle and yank it round. It begins to move with loud squeaks and we see the rope dangle down into the blackness. We have to wait awhile to get our breath back before heaving the handle in the other direction so that the rope rolls itself up around the revolving arm high above our heads, leaving the hook attached to the rope's end dangling above the well's mouth.

"I know what, let's hide it."

"What?"

"Let's hide the well, cover it over so the grown-ups can never find it."

We have to find long branches and drag them over to criss-cross the hole. It's a difficult and dangerous task and Mummy calls me in before we have finished. The next day, and the next, Max and I toil long and hard, finding twigs to cover the branches, leaves and handfuls of grass to throw over the twigs.

Every time I have to go in, Mummy wants to know how on earth I got so dirty, but I don't say anything. She scrubs my hands, wipes my face with a flannel, and gives up with my dungarees.

Finally Max is satisfied that we've finished.

"You mustn't tell anyone. Just you and me know, if anyone comes in here, they'll fall into our trap and we've captured them."

Washing my face before teatime Mummy asks what I've been up to. If only I could tell her. Perhaps she knows. My face feels warm; I can't look into her eyes.

"Nothing."

"Well you've been a long time doing nothing and got very dirty doing it."

She does know. Grandma puts the plate of jam sandwiches on the table in front of me.

"Been having a lovely time dear?"

I search her face but she gives nothing away.

The next morning I go to the well before Max comes round. The camouflage is still there. Shall I take it away? Max would be cross. But what if one of the adults falls in? Max said it would serve them right, especially the ones from the houses round the yard that shout at us for just playing. A picture comes up of the thin man with the brown suit stepping onto our trap and hurtling downwards, falling with a plop at the bottom. I turn away and go inside.

Luckily Mummy is taking me out, so I don't have to play with Max or face the well. Neither of us plays there for days.

I'm showing Jacky how to balance my wooden bricks on top of each other. We're in the kitchen where Mummy and Auntie Sally are having their chat over the washing and a cup of tea, their headscarves bobbing up and down. Something in their conversation makes my hand stop in mid-air.

"Wasn't it terrible about Mrs. Hodgekiss breaking her ankle last night?"

"Yes, that backyard is such a state. I'm not surprised she fell over; it must have been one of those holes in the ground."

"Do you know she was stuck out there all night and nobody heard? Poor old soul. What was she doing out there in the dark anyway? She knows it's dangerous with the well and everything."

Keep head low; hope Jacky doesn't draw attention to us. Mrs. Hodgekiss is one of the old ladies who shout at Max and me. She has a pinched nose and hair in a tight bun. She'd wandered out into the yard, through into our secret place, stepped onto the trap and fallen into the depths of the well. She must have crawled out and lain on the ground, exhausted and unable to move with her broken ankle, or cry out, knowing that her helplessness had been caused by us. They will all know.

My head droops; I won't ever look up.


12

The hedge towers over my head, its bright green leaves almost touching the clear blue sky. My neck arches as I keep my head twisted back to focus on the highest point that curves over and away from me. On either side of me the thick bank of greenery stretches to infinity. It's just as I imagined Golders Green, though I never thought it would be as high as this when they told me we were coming.

We're standing on the pavement outside Golders Green; Mummy, Grandma, Daddy Bender and I; excited because we've arrived after such a long journey on the train, the bus and finally in the taxi, impatient to see Jonathan and all the aunts and uncles.    Here they come, Auntie Daisy first, trotting down the path from the house leading to the gate in the hedge.    Good, Jonathan must be here somewhere.  Auntie Daisy, flashing smile, pretty face, dark wavy hair, reaches Mummy and they hug each other tightly.

"Darling, it's wonderful you've come."

Auntie Minnie is next, a little fairer than Auntie Sally, a little rounder in the face, a little plumper, even prettier and ever more gushing.  Mummy looks small beside both of them.

The uncles.  Short, stubby, straight, strict Uncle Bernard, a slight smile playing below his bristling moustache.  Jonathan is certainly here somewhere.  Uncle Reggie, tall and handsome who, once the kissing, hugging and handshaking subsides, stands behind Auntie Minnie, his arm around her waist; then young Uncle Bernard, dark locks of hair, dark eyes, quiet voice, shyly standing behind the others.

The aunts all kiss me; uncles rub their hands in my hair.  Hold on to Mummy's dress.  Auntie Miriam tells me how big I am.  Legs surround me, chattering goes on above me, quietens down when someone says, "Here he is."

Uncle Jack steps from the house, wearing a smart light blue uniform and marches through the crowd to us, kisses Grandma on the cheek, Mummy on the forehead, swirls me high over his head. Through his dark sleek hair I can see some of his round head showing through like Daddy Bender's does.  When he kisses me his black moustache tickles like Daddy's.  He's lofting me skyward again and holding me there with strong arms.  His brown eyes smile up at me, my head feels giddy.  He lowers me to the ground; his uniform feels rough against my skin.

Legs around me once more as Uncle Jack is engulfed by everyone wanting to kiss him, shake his hand.  The noise subsides once more; the legs clear a passage.

Daddy Bender stands alone, a little further down the pavement, clearing his throat, his head high, his watch-chain glinting in his waistcoat pocket.  Uncle Jack paces to him.  They clasp hands and shake them for a long time.  Daddy Bender puts his hand to Uncle Jack's cheek and pats it.

"God bless you son."

Arms go round each other's shoulders.

Everyone starts to move towards the house inside the hedge. At last I'll see Jonathan. Why are Grandma and Auntie Miriam crying?

13

The cat stares sedately back and slowly winks at me, opens its mouth and gives a dainty meow.

Your pink tongue and white teeth flash out brilliantly against your black fur. I've seen you before, but never sitting on my wall. I often sit on there, just on that spot, my feet dangling but not quite touching the ground, watching for anything that might go on, or for anyone who might go past. Sometimes nothing happens. Sometimes the milkman comes by with his navy peaked cap and blue-and-white striped apron, his milk bottles clinking and his crates clanking on the milk cart pulled by his big brown horse with the blinkers and long nose-bag. The milkman always sounds cheery and says hello to me. The horse follows him clopping up the street and when the milkman stops to take some milk bottles to our doorstep, or Jacky's doorstep the horse stops to put its head down and munches deep inside its nosebag. When they get to the cattle-grid, the milkman takes hold of the reins and pulls the horse and cart round in a circle; then he jumps into the front of the cart, shouts 'giddeyap' and off they go, clopping, clinking and clanking down the street. Sometimes green and brown jeeps come along crowded with singing men with uniforms to match the jeeps, bumping across the cattle-grid into the Common. The men wave and shout 'Hi kid' when they come past and shower me with chocolate bars and packets of chewing gum. Once the tall old man in the long brown raincoat got his walking-stick caught in the cattle-grid and spent ages trying to get it out, twisting and turning it, muttering and grumbling, looking at me angrily so that I got off the wall and went into the back-yard to play.

Now you're on the wall and I'm in the street. Your eyes are so yellow, your fur so black. Another meow, such a pink tongue, such a gentle plea; yes, I'll come and cuddle you, stroke your soft fur. We haven't been so close before have we? I can touch you now and look right into your face; what long whiskers.

Cat rears up, front paws reach out, long sharp claws spurt out from the ends; a snarling, spitting, vicious devil lunges. Head back, but no escape. Jagged nails rip down cheeks. Yellow globes of spite flash at me; crooked hind legs and long twisted tail disappear over the wall and into the bushes.

Hands to burning, throbbing face. Run. Scream for Mummy.

Gentle bathing and dabbing with warm moist cotton wool does little to take away the searing pain, only mops the blood. My scratched face is too sore for the piece of chocolate to be rubbed on it; even popping it in my mouth makes it no better.

Later, Daddy Bender takes me by the hand to look for the cat, shouts 'shoo' at it when he sees it.

"Just wait till I catch that cat."

I just want to get away from it.


## 16

"I'm going to show you something special today."

It's hard to keep up with Daddy Bender, my hand clasped inside his, and to look up at him as we walk in the wrong direction. He doesn't look down, just continues his steady, straight-ahead pace along Park Street. What is Daddy Bender going to show me that's so special? Aren't we going to the Common today? Why are we going this way? Are we going to the nursery school? I'm too breathless running alongside the tree-trunk legs to ask any questions; in any case Daddy Bender is telling me things.

"Everything will be different after the war. We shall be back in London; your Daddy will be home and we can start again. But first we have to beat Hitler. Poor London; you don't know what he's doing to it. That's why we came here, to get you away from the bombing. The Germans will never find us here."

Daddy Bender likes to tell me these things. It's important to listen to him, even if I can only get vague pictures.

We've arrived at the bottom of Park Street, turned into the wideness of High Street lined with regiments of trees, shops, stranded bicycles. Cars and lorries hurtle by, people chatter past, a sudden iron rumble of a train thunders over the bridge as we pass underneath it, making me jump. I hold onto Daddy Bender tightly as we walk. People say good morning to him and he raises his cap to each of them. Round a corner, a different road, a high wall, a long building. We stop.

"Here we are."

He pushes at a great wooden and glass structure. It starts to turn like a roundabout. We step inside as it's moving, stumble round and find ourselves in a vast silent room.

The ceiling is high, high above me, with patterns on it and long lights hanging down from it. As we take a few steps, my feet sink into an enormous expanse of red carpet with flowers on it. Pictures hang on the walls, of horses, of men in red coats sitting round a table, of a sailing ship.

We are alone in this place. Daddy Bender takes off his cap puts his hands on the back of my neck and shoulders. A black-suited man emerges from a doorway opposite and glides across the carpet, not towards us but looking over in our direction.

"Good morning Mr. Bender sir."

Daddy Bender greets him.

"This is my great-grandson."

"Aha."

The man wheels over and comes to us; holds his hand out to me. I hand him mine and he shakes it.

"And what's your name, young man?"

I hesitate; tell him as the hand on my shoulders encourages.

"My grand-daughter's son."

"Ah; and how old are you?"

I stand as high as I can.

"Three."

The man and Daddy Bender stand talking about air raids, Churchill, the Americans, while I press my toes into the carpet, watching it bounce up and down, feeling like grass under my feet. The man laughs at something, makes a slight bow with his head to Daddy Bender, winks at me and swirls on through the room to another door.

"You haven't said hello to the bear yet."

Hands turn me round to face back the way we had entered. Something leaps inside my chest, sharp tingles run through my body, sweep out of my head and neck, eyes bulge, mouth drops. Towering above me, reaching out massive paws, its jaws open in a snarl, stands a great brown bear. Shivers zip up and down me, feet stick to carpet, eyes fix on rows of yellow teeth. Daddy Bender pats the bear on the head.

"He can't hurt you. See, he's stuffed. He's here because this is the Bear Inn. Here, touch him, feel his fur, just like a teddy bear."

But he's not just like a teddy bear. Perhaps he can't hurt me, but he would if he could, using those paws to catch me, those claws to tear at me, those teeth to bite pieces from me. My hands will remain firmly by my side.

Daddy Bender lifts me up and holds me close to his chest.

"I'll look after you, don't you worry."

I gaze at the bear, safe from him in Daddy Bender's arms, wanting to show that I can touch him, knowing that I can't. We walk back through the revolving doors and out into the street.

The bear doesn't follow.

### 17

Down Park Street, just past the cottages is the hedge, then the path veering away off the road. We never go up here. Step carefully, path feels uneven under my feet, goes up steeply. Long twigs and leaves sticking out from the scraggly hedge brush against me as I try to keep to the side. The way ahead is dark, seems to go nowhere. Go back. No; go on a little further just to see what's at the end. Getting steeper, rougher. Stop. I can hear myself breathing, feel my thumping heart. A ringing noise floats over from behind the hedge. It's not the end, only a corner where the ground becomes flatter, smoother and where the path curves round and leaves the hedge. I can go fast now.

It's light here, a sudden open space. A concrete square of ground surrounded by high buildings of dark red brick, full of gloomy windows, topped by tall chimney-pots, pointed towers and a large clock. Above them all, glinting in the sunlight, a bell hangs from a rooftop archway, sending out a constant, single ringing call.

In the middle of the courtyard there is a small metal drain cover, like a tiny cattle-grid. By standing on it with both feet and rocking from side to side the drain cover clicks in time with the bell. Next I turn round and round on the drain, faster and faster so that sky and buildings revolve like a spinning-top. My head feels strange. I stop, but the buildings keep going round. The bell has stopped ringing. I try to keep my eyes on it to catch it starting again but that's moving too, gradually slows down and stops in one place.

A shuffling, fidgeting noise. Where's it coming from? Behind me. Turn.

A row of black-clad figures has lined up along one side of the yard. Pale faces show through holes in the top of the black garbs, framed by wide white collars. They are all the same. More figures, all exact copies, are streaming out of the building; clockwork dolls joining the others moving around the square. I am completely surrounded by silent staring faces.

The drain cover rocks a little. I can just poke the toe of my shoe into one of the gaps. It gets stuck. Standing like this is quite difficult. Perhaps if the bell starts ringing again they will all go away and I can be back home.

Footsteps are coming towards me. Two pairs of black shoes stop in front of the drain. Black flowing robes, hanging in folds like the black-out curtains, soar upwards. White capes peak out above me. The faces of two wrinkled smiling ladies are looking down at me.

"Hello little fellow."

A soft lilting voice floats down.

"And where have you come from?"

I look round me, as far as I'm able without moving feet. The path has gone.

"Well, it's lovely that you've come to visit us. Shall we go and say hello to the sisters and then perhaps it will be time to go back home."

A hand appears from somewhere inside the black folds. The fingers are bent and lumpy; feel strange fastened around my hand.

I'm drawn away, with a little difficulty from my drain, towards one of the waiting lines. Faces look down to me; names are given. The faces are not all the same, some young, some old, all smiling, all sisters. They are crowding around me, no longer standing in orderly straight rows, bunched up, blocking out the sky, saying nothing, making little sighing, singing sounds. My eyes are filling up. I put my head down.

A rustle of material and one of the faces separates itself from the jumble, lowers itself so that I can see her without looking up. A clear, twinkling eyed pretty face whose voice is a bell.

"Now we're going to find your mummy. Would you like that?"

A nod.

"Good, then you come with me."

Her hand is soft.

An opening appears in the black swarm. She and I walk steadily through it to the edge of the yard where a gap in the hedge reveals the path.

"Well now, I do believe we've found her."

Striding up the path from around the corner is one of the sisters; just behind her, emerging from the shadows is Mummy, wearing her apron over her slacks, her dark hair flowing and bouncing; stumbling, running to find me. I hang on to the hand I have.

"Thank you for looking after him; I didn't even know he'd gone."

"You're welcome, it's been a pleasure. We don't get many visitors; I think he's quite enjoyed himself here."

My sister puts her face down to me again.

"Would you like to stay with us?"

I nod, and she and Mummy and I walk around meeting all the nuns again until everyone is laughing and the bell rings. The three of us watch while they form back into lines, file into the building smiling and waving goodbye.

## 19

The smile seems to crack open my face. I can't remember when I last smiled; it hurts when I do it now but this is something to smile about, or at least to stop feeling miserable about; except that I'm up here and he's down there.

I stand balanced on the window sill, Mummy propping me against the pane, my mouth and one hand making little smudges on the glass, the other waving until my wrist aches and I have to change hands. Down there in the street below me, Jonathan returns my waves with both hands, his head thrown back in his push chair, his dark hair flopping around as he bounces up and down, kicking his heels against the foot-rest, laughing with excitement and shouting up at me. Auntie Daisy and Auntie Minnie are there too, standing behind the pushchair, looking up at us, blowing kisses.

It feels as though I can almost touch him, yet this window keeps him so far away, shuts me off from him. I wish I could be down there, hug him, and take him for a walk on the Common. But I'm stuck up here; all I can do is smile and wish, feeling happy and miserable at the same time.

Feeling miserable started days ago, when I woke one morning feeling some itching round my neck, warmth around my face. Mummy had sat me on her lap and looked at my neck when I told her, then undone my pyjama jacket and had a good look at my chest. She'd gone downstairs and I heard her talking to Grandma who then came upstairs with Mummy to have a second look.

"Yes I think you're right, we'd better call Doctor Blake."

And Doctor Blake had come; a cheerful man with a deep voice and a large brown leather bag with all kinds of things inside. He also inspected my neck and chest, put a glass tube under my armpit, pulled

36

my ears roughly and said 'measles.' I could see nothing in his face to tell me what he meant by this, but I felt a strange and unpleasant sinking sensation in my stomach as soon as he said the word. It didn't go away even when Grandma smiled; nodding as though she had known all the time, and Mummy clapped her hands together, shouted out the word gleefully and hugged me to her.

When the doctor had gone Mummy took me upstairs, put me back to bed and drew the curtains.

"You mustn't get the light in your eyes when you have measles, it will hurt you."

I realized I had to hide from the measles. What would they do to me? I couldn't escape from them; I couldn't even tell what they looked like. I just stayed in bed trying to be as still as possible.

Later I began to feel the measles creep all over my body. They made me feel hot and prickly, and everything began to itch. I felt heavy and tired, giddy even lying in bed, altogether peculiar.

As I ran my hands over my body it seemed as though it no longer belonged to me. Measles now owned me.

Sounds still floated up to me from the kitchen, seeming more distant and dreamlike than usual. I could picture them just the same; perhaps even more clearly. Mummy bustling about, talking and laughing, Grandma large and ponderous, mixing food into a deep bowl, churning it round and round with a wooden spoon, dipping her finger in and giving it a lick. I imagined Daddy Bender out in the backyard, chopping wood, mending or making something, hammering, planing, and chiselling at a block of wood until it formed into some new and recognizable item. None of this made me want to be with them, I just felt my heaviness.

Sometimes, Mummy or Grandma would come up and sit on my bed, holding my hand; but I just let it flop, not really caring whether she was there or not.

They came in together later on; Grandma sat me up, Mummy put the light on and walked across the room. She took hold of the mirror that hung on the wall from a loop of string tied to the end of its wooden handle. The mirror part was round and as big as my head; she brought it over to me and put it in front of my face.

"What do you think of your funny old measly face?"

Measles stared back at me. They were angry red spots covering every part of my face. I hadn't noticed before, but then I realized that these spots were all over my chest, tummy, arms and legs. Grandma helped me to examine them.

"Try not to touch them. Mummy's going to put something on to soothe them."

Not touching them was going to be hard as they itched all the time.

A bottle of pink liquid appeared in Mummy's hand. She shook some drops of it onto a pad of cotton wool and dabbed it onto some spots on my arm. Ah, the coolness on my hot skin, the relief from the itching! As I watched, the pink blobs turned into a white chalky powder. More dabbing, more coolness, more relief, more pink-into-chalk; until I was covered all over with white blotches. Another look in the mirror at an even stranger face. Would it stay like that?

The treatment with the magic lotion continued morning and evening. I couldn't say its name properly and made Mummy laugh each time I tried. I practiced when she wasn't there and thought I had it right, but I simply couldn't get my tongue round it when she was there.

After a few days the spots turned pinker and began to fade, to disappear altogether until it was hard to find any.

This morning when I woke up, I had a good search. The measles had gone. Mummy had drawn the curtains back at last.

"I've got a surprise for you, look who's here. Wave to him. You can only see him from here; you're not quite better yet and we don't want Jonathan to catch the measles from you, do we?"

No, I wouldn't like him to get all those spots, so however much I want to be down there I shall just smile and wave.

The aunts call up.

"Goodbye darling, wish you better soon."

They wave and walk off back down the street, Jonathan twisting his head back to see me.


20

It must be a watercress day. The garden rake over Daddy Bender's shoulder and the tin box under his arm are the signs.

"Are we going to the river?"

"Yes."

"Can I help you get the watercress?"

"If you're careful and don't go too close to the edge."

"Can we go and see the horse?"

"We'll see."

"Have you got some sugar for him?"

We are halfway down Park Street. Daddy Bender stops and peers up into the clear blue sky, shades his eyes.

"See the aeroplane, up there, by itself; it might be your Great Uncle Jack."

It's little more than a speck in the sky buzzing along. How can Great Uncle Jack be up there in such a tiny aeroplane? How did he get up there?

We watch until the speck disappears over the trees, leaving a fading buzz in the memory.

"One of ours; it could be him. Don't you think you've got a brave uncle?"

"Yes."

And a clever one too.

We've reached the river, walk along it to the spot where part of it splits off and runs into a pool. Nobody else knows this place. Daddy Bender sets down the box and leans on the rake, gazing at the greenery floating in the pool.

"Can I get the watercress please?"

"Come along then. Hold the rake like this. Good. Now gently draw it back. Whoops."

The rake is heavier than it looks; droops down into the water instead of staying up straight like it does when Daddy Bender holds it. Get up. Hold the end of the pole against my chest, heave it up, pull it back; here it comes with a mass of greenery.

"Look at all my watercress."

Daddy Bender looks. He lifts the head of the rake and unravels the fronds, plops them back into the water.

"I'm afraid those are weeds; you've missed the watercress."

He takes the rake, dips it effortlessly into the pool, no splash, and gently draws it back, catching up another knot of greenery. He holds it, dripping, towards me.

"That's the watercress, see."

It looks exactly the same to me, but Daddy Bender carefully lifts it from the rake, deposits it in his box and returns to fish for more. How can he tell weeds from watercress? The box is soon full and Daddy Bender lets me carry it.

A different way home, past the gated field where we wait. The horse is at the other end of the field, head down munching grass. Daddy Bender clicks his tongue.

The horse lifts his head high, turns it to look at us and pauses for a moment so that he looks like a shining black statue. He's trotting over; cantering straight to us, his great body rippling, his mane bouncing, his hooves thumping the ground so that I can feel it going through me. Closer, filling everything up with his size. He can't stop; his power will burst through and crush us. No, he's slowing; trotting to show he was only pretending and can do anything he likes. He's at the gate, thrusting his head over the bars, enormous brown eyes rolling at me, nostrils flaring, teeth gnashing.

The horse nuzzles his head against Daddy Bender, who puts his hand into his pocket and pulls out a carrot, which the horse takes daintily and munches. Another nuzzle; this time a sugar-lump.

"Would you like to give it to him? Just hold your hand out flat like this otherwise he might think your fingers are to eat."

My hand is very flat. The horse puts his lips over the sugar-lump, hardly touching my hand apart from making it a little damp.

There is no more sugar or carrot, so I tear up handfuls of grass from the verge and offer it. This grass is coarse and dry, not like the rich green grass in the field; yet the horse is happy to take it from me.

Daddy Bender slaps the horse on the neck and it doesn't seem to mind. But the horse is my friend. He puts his head down to me, blows through his nose, nods and nudges me on the shoulder.

"Come along, it's time to go, we'll come and see him another day. Give him a pat on the nose."

I do, very gently, but the horse seems offended, turns his head away.

As we walk down the lane I look round to see him eyeing me sadly. A little further on and his hooves thunder away across the field.

### 21

"Come and help me fetch the bath in."

This could be a good thing to do, but does it mean I shall have to get in it? The soap always gets in my eyes and the water goes cold and I start to shiver when I stand up afterwards.

"Are you coming? I want to have a bath."

"Yes, coming."

Good, watching Mummy having a bath is alright.

I run into the kitchen where she is dragging the tin bathtub in from outside where it rests against the wall.

"Hold the handle on your end and lift it up."

The two of us manage to get the bath into the front room, and puffing and blowing, drop it onto the rug in front of the fire.

Backwards and forward we go from kitchen to bathtub, me carrying saucepans of cold water, Mummy with kettles of boiling water, pouring into the big oval vessel. At first the water only covers the bottom; then gradually creeps up the sides. It takes a long time before Mummy says it's enough and gets the wooden clotheshorse from the kitchen. She opens it out, sets it next to the bath and drapes a large white towel over its side facing the fire.

This is a better job; as Mummy gets undressed, I can fold her clothes and put them on the clotheshorse where they hang neatly in a colourful row ready for her when she's finished.

In she steps, sits down in the water carefully, folding herself up tidily, knees under her chin. Dark hair falling over her face, splashing herself so that droplets run around her shoulders and down her back. Grandma and Daddy Bender would look very big in that tiny tub. I know they do it because Daddy Bender grumbles about it. How do they get in?

Mummy keeps losing the soap, giggles as she searches for it, drops it again. It pops out of my hand when I wash her back with the bar of soap and we are both laughing when there's a knock at the door.

"Could you see to that dear? I expect it's the milkman."

Yes, I can do this; there's nobody else at home and I'm the only one to guard Mummy and do jobs for her. I can just reach the door-handle now if I stand on tiptoes and stretch up. Turn the handle, pull it towards me.

The milkman stands there in his striped apron and peaked cap. Behind him his horse clops to a halt and munches busily, nosing inside the long sack that droops from its reins onto the ground.

The milkman always smiles at me and waves, but this is the first time we have had a conversation.

"Hello, is your Mummy in?"

When he comes at other times and Mummy answers the door to him, she gives him some money from her purse. I think her purse is on the mantelpiece over the fire and I mustn't reach up there.

I give him a good nod.

"Yes, in here."

I walk backwards into the room. He stands hovering on the doorstep for a moment looking down at me, his pencil sticking out from under his cap, jingling money in his apron pouch, then steps right inside the room after me.

A frantic shriek, wild splashing, wooden clattering. Turn. Mummy standing up in the tub reaching out desperately, clotheshorse crashing to the floor, white towel flying into the air. Turn again; milkman frozen still, mouth open with spluttering noises coming out, face turning bright red; backing out of the room, pulling the door closed as he steps outside.

I can't turn round again. As I stand looking blankly at the door my face feels a burning sensation coming over it. Behind me, silence; muffled explosion; great guffaws, and as I slowly manage to twist around, Mummy covered from eyes to knees in the white towel shaking with gusts of crying; no, of laughter.

It's hard to move towards her, my legs feel heavy and wobbly; when I get there I can only stand in front of her, hands by my side, while she keeps her face hidden, giggling in a strange way. Then, peeping at me from the folds of the towel, she bursts into explosive chuckles once more. As she dries herself, dresses and we clear up the debris and empty the bath, she keeps lapsing into fits of laughter. When we take the tin tub outside, she tells Auntie Sally and they collapse into each other's arms, shoulders shaking wildly, squealing with mirth, taking no notice of me apart from the occasional glance that makes my face feel hot again.

The milkman calls a few days later. I stand behind Mummy clutching her skirt when she goes to the door. They say nothing about it, but Mummy keeps her head low and the milkman speaks in a much quieter, less cheerful tone than usual. I keep my eyes away from the milkman's face.

*Untitled # 1, Roméo Savoie, 2012*

# Elizabeth Blanchard

## The ASDIC Operator
## (an excerpt)

*Department of Veterans Affairs*
*October 29, 1945*

*To: District Administrator, Saint John, N.B.*
*Attention: C.M.O.*
*Subject: RE- V-39347 – Robichaud, Calixte*

> *We are today in receipt of a communication from Dr. N.H. Scott, our Sub District Office, Sydney, N.S., requesting accommodation for the above mentioned following his discharge from the Service. The diagnosis shown is Minimal Tuberculosis, and we would appreciate if you would advise when accommodation is available*

*D. Mullins , M.D.,*
*Chief Medical Officer*

I can tell by the trundle of the gurney that the floor surface is irregular, that certain tiles must be uneven at the seams, probably due to frost shift over the years. The building is old; I can smell its age. Beneath the strong smell of disinfectants and liniments, beneath the uneasy scent of sweat soaked sheets, even beneath the tang of Nurse Mable's body odour when she leans over me to wash my rib cage, I can smell the mould, imagine it growing in damp crevices where shrunken wooden frames have pulled away from the stone masonry. Having spent four years on a cork of a ship, the scent is familiar; like an uncomfortable acquaintance you would rather avoid but that keeps showing up. Even when on furlough, I would sometimes wake in a strange bed and smell it before I opened my eyes, as though mildew had infiltrated the layers of my skin.

The sound of the rolling wheels beneath me changes abruptly, a slightly higher pitch. The flooring in this part of the corridor must be different, newer maybe, but from where I'm lying the ceiling and the walls don't look any different. The skirt of Nurse Mable's uniform rustles against the side of the gurney. Her breath is audible as she wheels me down the hall, the muscles in her chest most likely straining under the weight of those heavy breasts. I'm guessing by the size of the knuckles in her hand and the length of her fingers clamped to the side-railing that she must have been a smaller woman at one point, just as I, at one point, was a bigger man.

We come to a stop. Nurse Mable moves to the head of the gurney out of my line of vision and I hear a door open. She rolls me inside the "treatment room".

Another nurse wearing a surgical mask and white cap moves up to my right and leans over me, her almond-shaped eyes make me want to reach up and undo the ties behind her head so I can see her mouth.

"Mr. Rawbichaud." The way she draws out the first syllable of my name tells me she doesn't speak French; the look in her eyes tells me she's new at this, "Mr. Rawbichaud, we're going to transfer you to the table. Just relax, let us do the work." Both nurses grab the sheet under my hips and shoulders. Nurse Mable counts: "One, two, three." The ease with which they lift my body embarrasses me; frailty has never been my strong suit.

"Lay him on his left side," a male voice says from a corner of the room I can't see. I hear the legs of a chair grate against the tile floor; I hear him clear his throat. The thick guttural sound makes me want to cough; I resist by swallowing hard several times.

The doe-eyed nurse skillfully removes my pyjama top, lays me on my right side and brings my right hand up to rest under my head; her hands are soft against my chest. I feel the need to say something, to hear the sound of my own voice rise up to theirs.

"What time do you get off work?" I force a wink and a smile at the doe-eyed one.

The sound of my voice makes her eyes shift back to my face, but my words don't register, she's thinking only of the task at hand. It suddenly occurs to me that she's nervous.

"Slide the bolster up." The doctor's voice has moved from the corner of the room and is directly behind me now. "Higher, open the space between the second and third rib. No. Look. Here, where my finger is."

The doe-eyed one slips the cigar-shaped pillow I'm lying on up towards my armpit causing my spine to arch awkwardly which triggers an unexpected spasm and I begin to cough. The young nurse steps back and thrusts a square piece of gauze in my face at arm's length. I clutch the gauze making a fist, and move it to my lips which are now spraying saliva and sputum. I feel the growing succession of spasms in my chest that have me gasping for air, every muscle in my torso seizing until I'm no longer sure if I'm coughing or vomiting. Curled up on the table, my head near the edge, I look down at the nurse's feet, at the white of her soft-sole shoes, trying to calm the muscles in my chest and in my throat, my cough now sounding more like a deep-throated gag. I will myself to relax, think of old man Ferguson. "Look toward the horizon, lad", he would bark from the bridge whenever he caught a man heaving over the side of the ship or into a bucket. "The horizon, man, the horizon!" that imaginary line between sea and sky upon which a sick man anchors his hopes of calmer waters. I never did believe it did much other than force a man to raise his head away from his own troubles, but then again, I was one of the lucky ones who never got seasick.

The smell of iodine and alcohol with which they paint my exposed ribs stings my nose. I swallow hard not to cough again. The doctor is leaning over me from behind; he is explaining something to me, he calls me son. He is talking slowly and clearly, but his words don't stick, the exhausted muscles in my chest tug at my every thought; every breath aches. He is going to cut an opening in my skin and slip in a needle, a needle which will travel between my ribs into my chest but stop short of my lung, a needle through which air will be pushed into the gap between the inner wall of my chest cavity and my lung, air that will fill up and swell the discreet gap, causing my lung to deflate like a balloon. This, he assures me, will help, will stop the growth of the tuberculi. "A collapsed lung will allow the cavity in your lung to heal," he says. "The tuberculi can't breed in a collapsed lung." The pun, which I will only come to fully understand with time, puts a smile in his voice, I can hear it and see it in the corresponding rise of the nurse's cheeks behind her mask. But her eyes tell me hers is but a reflective smile, a submissive response. I want to reach up and grab the doctor's shoulders, look him in the eye to see what kind of man he is, see if I can trust him, let him know that he is no different a man than me. But I am at a disadvantage here, in his space. Unlike on board ship, the man assigned to me does not in turn need me for his own survival; the balance of power is off keel.

I feel only the first needle he uses to dull the area, I don't feel the second but I imagine it pushing through my skin, finding its way

47

between my rib bones, inserting air into a new found space, broadening a gap in my chest cavity I never knew existed, causing my lung to pull away from my chest wall and collapse. Goddam! The pain is sharp. My breath quickens but to no avail; I can't inhale. My mind panics, claws at consciousness as it begins to slip, then fall, I imagine, into the gap expanding inside my chest.

I sailed through the gap over the mid-Atlantic before they closed it, before it became part of the lore that ordinary seamen inherited along with the propensity to function when wet and exhausted. I sailed through it, or rather under it, more than once. Maurice was the one who pointed it out to me one night during my first crossing. "Écoute," he said, pointing to the sky, a cigarette hanging between his oil-stained fingers, the same oil that had soaked the heavy cotton of his dungarees into a permanent stain, the stink of it so strong off these stokers you could smell petrol on their breath.

The big mechanic from Sainte-Anne des Monts, Québec, always spoke French to me. I had just finished my two hours on in the Asdic house when I met *Gros Mo*, as the men had christened him, on the upper deck. He had finished his shift in the boiler room. He held my gaze until I looked up at the black sky and back at him, not knowing what the hell he was getting at.

"T'entends-tu? Écoute."

I listened, but could only hear the push of the large propellers and the heave and creak of the ship's hull. When I said nothing, he turned his eyes away to the horizon knowing that I would eventually understand. He brought the cigarette to his lips and took a slow long drag as if the smoke were sweet. "Icitte, c'est l'silence qui fait peur", he said in a quiet voice, as though he were no longer speaking to me. Silence isn't something you pay much mind to when you're young. At the time I thought Gros Mo was being philosophical, warning me not to isolate myself, not to cut myself off from others. I appreciated the thought, read it as the advice of a concerned 29 year-old fatherly figure that had decided to take me under his wing because I was the only other Frenchy on the ship. But I came to understand that at sea, silence wasn't an abstract notion, it was a solid in the pit of your stomach that had never been there before, or maybe that you had never noticed. The air gap was a space over the North Atlantic Ocean where Coast-Command planes couldn't reach, a hole in the sky that swallowed up the sound of allied aircraft. Its boundary, beginning when the drone of the last twin-engine plane faded, fluctuated with the boldness of the pilot; the young and cocky ones pushing it a bit further every trip. But in the end, it is the silence that defined the borders of the gap, the silence that tightened our muscles and quickened our breath at the very thought that it, the silence, would settle from the sky onto the surface and calm a wild sea, making us all the more vulnerable. A silence that had us listening, not for the sound of planes above our heads coming from the other side of the gap, but for the white wash of a shallow steel shell slicing the hull beneath our feet, the soft sound of incoming death.

Death, at least the threat of it, travelled beneath us, quietly and freely. Listening for its echo was one of my first duties on the ship. As one of the three Asdic operators on board, I spent much of my first crossings in the Asdic house, a small hut mounted on the bridge of the ship. Wedged in among the wires between the large compass and the collapsible bunk the captain had fitted to the wall, I methodically swept a 2,000 yard radius of sea beneath us with high frequency sound beams. Audible pings emitted horizontally from a dome fastened to the keel of the ship, travelled in half-moon arcs in search of objects off of which the sound could bounce and return as an echo. With one hand on the controller and the other holding up a headphone to my right ear, I would listen intently for that echo, following in my mind's eye the vibration of the ping as far out as possible until it slipped out of my reach and faded into the depths. Then I would shift the beam five degrees to port and ping again, until I had swept from bow to stern, repeating the ritual all over again on the starboard side. After an hour, when fatigue set in, especially at night, I would sometimes catch myself leaning forward and holding my breath as I travelled with the ping through dark waters out to edge, hanging there in the silence longer than necessary, imagining that if I turned my head, I could see the slick line of an *unterseeboot* following us, quietly, undetected, just beyond the arc of my beam. It is in these moments I understood how silence swells fear, brings it to life, gives it a shape and a form that presses on your arteries causing your heart to pump harder and your lungs to shrink to the point where you feel you can't breathe. It is in moments like these I understood why men like Gros Mo chose to intern themselves in the belly of the ship under back-bending work and battened hatches. Their minds, gratefully distracted by the clank and the heat and the stink of the boiler room, need not think of or listen for or worry about what moved beneath them.

I open my eyes to the sound of Nurse Mable's voice asking me how I feel. "It'll be better next time," she says matter of fact pushing my gurney down a corridor that I don't recognize, "next time, you'll know what to expect." I breathe in shallow and quick breaths only because I am afraid to inhale deeply, afraid of the pain inside my chest, afraid that whatever lung I have left in my chest won't take in air I need.

"Hang on," Nurse Mable says as she braces herself and pushes the gurney through a set of swinging doors into a large white ward stained with the scent of sickness. Along both walls are two rows of hospital beds, wrapped in washed-out sheets clinging to the slender forms hidden beneath them. Above the beds stretch tall narrow windows framed in wooden casings and draped in dull white curtains that blend into the colour of the wall. The sound of spasmodic coughing coming from the bed nearest the door catches in my throat and I swallow hard. Nurse Mable wheels me to the bed at the far end of the ward, slides the gurneys between the wall and the bed and motions to a tall broad-shouldered nurse across the way who is laughing with an orderly dressed in white, his black hair slicked away from his forehead under a shiny layer of pomade.

"Miss Brody," Nurse Mable says sharply.

Reluctantly, the tall nurse interrupts her conversation, strides over and stands on the opposite side of the bed to which I've just been assigned. Leaning across the bed, she grabs the sheet beneath my shoulder and my hips as does Nurse Mable who nods.

"One, two, three."

Both women grunt on the count of three and I am again lifted from my gurney as though I were suspended in a hammock, and quickly transferred to the bed.

Nurse Mable slides the gurney out between the bed and the wall and moves up next to my bed, shoving her hands into the small pockets of a white knit sweater that doesn't quite wrap around her broad hips.

"You must lie flat on your back, Mr. Robichaud. One pillow only. You must not sit or stand, until the doctor says you can. If you need to pee, one of the nurses will bring you a bedpan. You will be helped to the bathroom once a day."

My chest hurts bad and my heart is flailing wildly as though it's no longer anchored in place. I bring both hands to my breast bone to contain it; the expression on Nurse Mable face changes at the sight of me clutching my chest. She leans over me and lowers her voice. "Adhesions in the pleural cavity cause greater discomfort," she wraps her fingers around my forearm and squeezes, "the first time is always the worst."

Her last line strikes a raw chord, reminds me of the damp nights spent in a cramped messdeck listening to rating Ed Blonsky describe his carnal conquest from previous shore leaves. The longer the time at sea, the more lust-ridden and wishful his stories became, inviting satisfied grunts and tired erections from off-duty men stretched out in hammocks, desperate for sleep. Blonsky's favourite line, which never failed to elicit the raunchiest laughs, was always the same: *the first time is always the worst, luv.* The older guys all took turns yelling at him to stop yapping "stop yapping you horny little bastard." I, on the other hand, thought it funny, and was secretly grateful that it kept my mind off things until sleep came. But the line no longer strikes me as funny, here, in this space of tall windows and thin men. Maybe it's because it sounds different when out of the mouth of a woman, or maybe because I'm on the receiving end making me feel like I'm the one who is about to be fucked.

"Was it your first fill?" The man in the next bed is lying on his side facing me, both hands, palms flat together, folded under his cheek. "I remember my first trip to the gas station, didn't much care for it. Not saying that the Doc didn't do a good job. No, not saying that, no. Now Doc Mullens is a good man, a right good man. I just didn't care much for the way it made me feel afterwards. You know what I mean. "

His protruding wrist bones are telling; he is even thinner that I am. The colour of his flesh is just a tone off that of the sheets and the wall. If he hadn't opened his mouth to talk, I probably wouldn't have noticed him.

"I was flat back for two months after the first treatments. Nurses had to hold me up when they finally let me out of bed, hold me up just like a little kid learning to walk from day one."

Nurse Brody and the orderly are now laughing over in the far end of the ward, both of them leaning near a large table covered in folded linen and wash basins. I can't hear what they're saying, but I recognize the complicity in their voices, a longing for intimacy expressed in a public space, remnants of wartime etiquette.

"When did you come in?"

He's still looking at me, the guy in the next bed. "Two days ago." My voice is weak compared to the knocking against my ribs.

"Where you been?"

I look at him. I don't quite understand the question.

"Where you been? Where were you stationed?"

Where had I been for the past four years? There are no signposts at sea. Once you lose sight of the horizon, there are no familiar markers to help you pinpoint your position. A man has to know in what direction he must travel to move forward, but where I come from setting a course is a luxury dictated to you by someone other than yourself. That's just how it is, that's just how it's always been. For a *Frenchman* growing up on the north shore of New Brunswick, keeping your head down is instinctive, an innate behaviour inherited from the men that came before you. I learned this as a boy working in the logging camps alongside men with twice the strength and half the patience. Life was something that you swung into and dragged, like driving a pulp hook into the end of a log. So when I took to the sea, it never occurred to me to look up to the stars to get my bearings, I took my cues from the captain on the bridge.

Where *had* I been for the past four years? I'd ask the captain, but he isn't here.

## Man of Faith

I've been on the lookout for Jesus for some time now. I think I saw him on the bus this morning. His hair was short and he was clean shaven. Nevertheless, I recognized his aura, translucent and undulating. You could barely see it; I rubbed my eyes like people do when looking at the air above an asphalt road on a hot day. The man sharing the seat next to me had his nose in a book, his shoulders curled in towards his chest, his arms tucked tight in front of him, concerned that the sleeve of his down-filled coat should inadvertently touch mine. It was a shame really, had his body-language been more relaxed I would have pointed Jesus out to him. He would have been impressed.

On most days people avoid me because of my odor; my smell disturbs people, unsettles them. But I can't blame it on that today, because Jim snuck me into the staff shower early this morning. He said he'd do it if I let him watch. I only said yes because he's the easiest one to distract; I can always slip out without him seeing me. Besides, I knew it was his last week at the home, and that he wouldn't be back. He told me he had a new job lined up at a call center down on Dundas. I knew it was true because of the way he said I can't wait to leave this fucking hell-hole as he eyed me washing the folds of skin that hang beneath my arms.

I'd been thinking about Jim and the hole in hell when I spotted Jesus getting on the bus. I was surprised at the quality of the suit he was wearing, a fine double-breasted pinstripe, with a cuff. But then again, Jesus has always been about the unexpected. And what better way to go unnoticed. If I had a suit like that nobody would think twice about sitting next to me, I would blend in too. I really would have liked to talk to him, tap him on the shoulder and say something like what's with the suit anyway. It would have surprised him. I'm certain it would have made him smile. But in the end, with my belongings in plastic bags resting at my feet, I didn't move from my seat because I knew that the bus driver would have me off at the next stop, and it being awfully cold outside. This particular bus driver didn't swear at me, he even let me ride for free, only if I promised not to bother the others passengers.

The first time I met Jesus was in high school, he was sitting up on the rise behind the school on a Sunday night. It was the night the neighbours finally called the police on my father. I tried to hold him off until my mother barricaded herself in the bathroom. But you can't really do much in the presence of that kind of anger; it thins the blood, makes it run pale and fast. I squeezed out the basement window just as I heard the dull crack of a boot splitting the bathroom door from its hinges, like the sound of bones splintering.

As I said, that's the night I first spotted him, Jesus, up behind the school. He was sitting underneath the wild alders that ran the length of the graveyard fence. Actually, it was the tip of his cigarette I saw first, glowing, fading, glowing again, like a pinned firefly.

I sat down beside him because I didn't know what else to do. He put his cigarette to his lips, and turned to look at me, paused on intake when he caught sight of my face. He exhaled calmly, his eyes fixed on my cheekbone and ear, which had probably starting to clot by then. He slid his hand in his jacket pocket and handed me a cigarette. I shook my head, my mother hated cigarettes. We sat together for a long while. He talked about go-karts, fishing reels, and other things I can't remember. His voice was calm and slow. I never said much.

I had no idea who he was of course. It was my mother who first mentioned his name, the next day in the hospital. I had to lean over the bed railing in order to hear her. The stitches in her jaw made it hard for her to talk, sort of a whispering suck. It must have been Jesus, is what she said, when I told her why I hadn't come home the night before, Jesus taking care of my boy. I didn't say a word, just kept my mouth shut. She didn't need me making fun of her right there and then. I didn't even have the heart to tell her Jesus was a chain smoker.

Jesus didn't look much like a smoker this morning. I could see him near the front of the bus, talking to the young girl sitting next to him, her white t-shirt gone grey with side-walk dust, the tell tale sign of a runaway. At first she gestured flirtatiously when she spoke causing the silver bangles on her dirty wrist to slide up and down her forearm, while shaking her long matted hair. In the weighted grind of the bus's diesel engine, I watched the girl's shoulders settle and her head lean slightly towards Jesus as he spoke, looking first at her, then out the window, his hands resting in his lap, one finger rising slightly on occasion to bring attention to some point.

The girl reminded me of Maggie, except that Maggie wasn't a runaway; Maggie was a wanderer, a soul that had been cut from its mooring since birth is how she described herself. I first met Maggie at the flea market years ago, when I was a much younger man. I watched her paint henna tattoos on the tourists' ankles every Saturday morning in July, watched her dip a toothpick into a pod of henna, eucalyptus, and tea, and curl the Indian ink onto the thick skin of overweight woman in linen Capris, never once looking up at the amount of money they dropped in the canister next to the ink bowl as they twisted their ankles with squeals of delight. Maggie followed me back to my basement apartment after market one day. She took off her t-shirt and jeans, and sat on my mother's faded loveseat, her hands between her knees, her small breast fleshless against her ribs, like those dark skinned women on television holding their bloated-bellied babies in their laps.

"I can make you happy," Maggie said in a hoarse voice that reminded me of my mother on a morning-after, my father sitting across from her at the kitchen table, crying, the heel of his palms pushed up against his bloodshot eyes. It was a memory that had been dormant for a while. And like the tail of a kite caught in bramble, it tugged on other images; the wrinkled suits of the men hired by the bank for instance, who held an auction in our back yard six months after the police found my mother's body on the bathroom floor. I had already left home by then; my mother hadn't. I remember the low sky and the onlookers, their sleeves and shoulders glistening in the faint drizzle. I remember thinking that if I had a nice suit like those men, it would always be pressed. By the end of the afternoon, nobody had bid on my mother's red love seat.

Maggie loved to wrap her palms around a warm teacup and always cut her own hair. On good days at the market, she brought home asparagus and potatoes and made soup flavoured with tarragon. The night we played cribbage until dawn and smoked the stuff a guy in army fatigues had left in her canister for having drawn an eagle on his forearm, she told me that she had lied about being eighteen and how experiencing life was so much more important than school.

When I lost my job at the convenience store, she disappeared for two days and came home with a pair of dress pants and a suit jacket she bought for me at Value Village.

"I had them dry-cleaned." She said with a smile, holding up the hanger on which hung the neatly pressed suit. "Now you can get a job in an office with a filing cabinet, put your name up on the door instead of here," she tapped my chest.

I slipped the suit coat off the hanger, an unexpected wave of gratitude swelling in my chest. The paisley lining felt supple under my touch. The pants had cuffs and small gathers above the pockets. The coat pockets were neatly sewn shut, and the lapels were not too wide.

I wore the suit the following Saturday when I went to watch Maggie at the market. I was wearing it the evening I came home and found a large round-back man grunting over Maggie on the couch, his forehead against the armrest of the loveseat, her thin legs sprawled so wide I thought they would break at the hip. She saw me and waved me away, which was unnecessary because I moved quickly to my bedroom and shut the door. I checked an urge to hide under the bed as I had done many times in my father's house, because such things are not done by twenty-seven-year-old men in suits. Although relieved when I later heard the apartment door shut, I remained in my room until the next morning.

Maggie paid the rent at the end of the month, and the food we bought at the grocery store.

I spent more and more time in my room in the evenings, listening to the sounds of the men Maggie invited in. I suppose I could have stayed away at those times, hung out under the bypass where Maggie's friends gathered after dark. But I could not quiet the panic in my chest at the thought of Maggie in the grip of these strange men in my absence, perhaps it was the memory of the knuckle in my father's fist or the heel of his boot ringing my spine like a human tuning fork. I could not leave the apartment on those evenings when the men came. Out of habit, I would remove the screen of the small basement window from its soiled tracks and sit in silence on the edge of my bed, listening to the men's grunts and Maggie's involuntary gasps. I fought the urge to climb through the window, secretly worried that I would not fit or that my suit coat would snag on the frame on the way out. I sat in the dark, attentive to any changes in the thickness of the air, violence having its own specific density.

On occasion, after the men would leave, we would go out for pizza, or Maggie would order in. Her favourite was curried noodles from Spadina Garden. She never asked me why I stayed in the room when she earned her keep, for *earning her keep* is what she called it, but I knew from the way she hugged me tightly that she understood something of me that I did not understand myself.

I remember the night he returned; it was the fall of the year. Although a chill settled in my bones as I kept my customary watch in the darkness of my narrow room, I could never bring myself to completely close the window. It was the lack of noise that first drew my attention, that pulled me nervously away from my usual post on the bed's edge, my heart punching hard into my lungs making me catch my breath.

I pressed my ear to the door, afraid of the anger I might stir and bring down upon Maggie, upon myself, should I open it in an inopportune moment. It took a few minutes before I could discern any other sound than that of my own anxious breathing; then I heard him, not his words as much as the pitch and roll of his voice. He spoke softly, his warmth recognizable. He talked at length, ending with an inflection.

Maggie whispered something as if to answer his question, and when she did, I could tell she was no longer on the loveseat with him, but had moved to some other place in the room.

He spoke again, another inflection followed by a pause, a longer one.

I was so tempted to open the door, look at him, see if he had changed, wondered how he had found me again. I wanted so much to speak to him, so many questions that needed answers; I finally heard Maggie's voice respond. It sounded different, small, thin, like that of a young girl, a stranger really had I not known better.

Then I heard nothing, silence for the longest time; then movement, shuffling, footsteps, all muffled by the sound of my own breathing. I stood my ear, palms, and chest to the door long after I heard the apartment door close and knew that he and Maggie had left. I returned to sit on the edge of the bed only when I could no longer stand the stillness on the other side of the door. I waited for him to come back and fetch me, ashamed that I could not bring myself to open the door.

*** 

The door of the bus was barely shut behind me when I heard the engine roar away. The sidewalk was icy, my legs wooden and uncooperative. Jesus and the girl moved smoothly through the crowd. I tried to pick up the pace afraid that I might lose sight of them. A car honked as I stepped off the sidewalk to avoid a bunch of kids who kicked at my plastic bags. I was hoping I could catch up, hoping to ask him why, the night he left with Maggie, why hadn't he come back for me. Maybe he did and I wasn't there. I wanted to tell him that I had waited and waited and waited for him, but it was the policemen who came, who snapped the door off its hinges with their black boots, who pulled me down from the window, yelling and screaming, tearing my pants. One of the officers shouted at me, the one with his knee on my back, called me a pimp. Maggie was a minor, was what he said, just a fucking kid.

By the time Jesus and the girl turned the corner, I could feel threads of sweat running down my back. My clothes smell worse when I sweat too much; I am always careful not to sweat too much. They stopped; she turned to go her separate way just as I thought I would finally catch up to them. Listen to him, I wanted to shout to the girl, do you know who he is?

"Jesus Christ you old shit," a hand gripped my arm.

I recognized the voice instantly.

Jim's other hand took hold of my collar as I stumbled against the woman walking beside me. He jerked me in the other direction and pressed me up against the window of a bookstore. Jim pushed his face up into mine; his breath was sour in my nostrils.

"I've been looking for you all fucking morning. You got me in shit again with the head nurse, old man." Jim yanked my plastic bags out of my hand, "Where d'you think you're going with this crap." He hung on to my arm as he led me down the street in the opposite direction. I tried to pull away, to turn my head, to look back. "She's going to write me up, again. Fuck! like I needed this my last week of work." He squeezed tighter and pulled me close as he walked, "You're going in lock down, you crazy old bastard."

I tried to keep my feet moving fast. I didn't want to fall with Jim holding my arm, afraid he would drag me. I looked at the street sign, tried to memorize the name, the numbers on the buildings, so I could find my way back. Jim slipped on a patch of ice, "Sonofabitch." He loosened his grip for a moment and I turned. I could still see the girl, but she was alone now.

"C'mon," Jim snarled at me like a dog.

There was no need to stay. Jesus was gone. But I knew I would find him again, if not this week, then soon.

I am nothing if not a man of faith.

*26 Angels, David Skyrie, 2011*

# Noeline Bridge

## Triptych

In late December 1988 I travelled from Edmonton to London to attend my niece Kim's wedding. A few days later, I journeyed on to Amsterdam by bus, returning to Edmonton from Amsterdam's Schiphol airport. "Triptych" describes those three events.

### 1. Pentecostalist Wedding

On the morning of the wedding, rain was pelting the small window of the bedroom I shared with my sister Margaret. The wind was driving low clouds across the grey sky, and when I peered out into the grounds of the residence, I saw the large trees swaying in the storm. Going upstairs to Yvonne's apartment in my pyjamas and robe for coffee and breakfast, I saw Yvonne, already dressed for the wedding in a navy skirt suit, rushing around exhorting everyone to pray for good weather: "Pray for good weather! The Lord will hear our prayers." When not exhorting us, she was on the phone to the faithful, with the same plea. "Pray that the sun will shine for Kim's wedding!"

My niece Kim was being married in Staines Pentecostal Church, west of London. Her mother Margaret and her sister Jeanne-Marie, who was to be bridesmaid, had come from New Zealand for the occasion, and they and I, along with Kim, were staying with Yvonne. A member of the Staines church, Yvonne managed a seniors' residence, and had arranged the accommodations for us. Margaret's ex-husband, John, had flown from Africa, where he had been on safari, and was staying with a local Pentecostalist family, along with the groom, Lee.

Not believing that God intervenes in the weather, I refrained from adding my prayers, just going back downstairs to put on the woollen dress I had brought with me for the wedding, and to make up my face and pin my hair up into a chignon. As I went back upstairs, my raincoat over one arm, the shoulder strap of my suede purse over the other shoulder, and grasping my travel umbrella, I heard loud rejoicings from Yvonne's flat. "Hallelujah! The Lord has heard our prayers!" Yvonne's sitting room was now flooded with light, and, outside, the sun was shining through raindrops and the trees were still. Yvonne was back on the phone: "The Lord has heard us and made the sun shine for Kim's wedding!"

After a devastating experience with fundamentalism in my teens, I had always put as much distance as I could between myself and manifestations of fundamentalism, not easy to do when you have beloved relatives involved in it. Trying to ignore the outpourings of ecstasy, I placed my raincoat and umbrella on a chair in a far corner of the sitting room, and joined Margaret and Jeanne-Marie in Kim's bedroom for the practical task of helping the bride into her frock. Having been a bridesmaid three times before I was a bride, I could suppress my anxiety in lifting layers of lace over and down the wide circle of Kim's crinoline petticoat, helping set the lace and net veil on her brown hair, and arranging the short train of the dress behind her.

Yvonne's shout came from the sitting room: "The photographer's here! Where's the bride?" so we helpers scurried into the sitting room. John was there, looking suntanned from Africa and uncomfortable in a borrowed suit. As I greeted him, he complained, "This suit is awful. And my face has come out in spots since I came to England. Can you help me?" I couldn't help the suit but could help the spots: I scurried to my handbag to retrieve a makeup stick, which I carefully dabbed on the spots, with just enough time to replace it before Kim, moving slowing in her lace layers, the train following her, came into the room. I retreated to the edges, watching the wedding party group and regroup themselves for the photographer.

Then Yvonne, looking out of a window, called, "The cars are arriving! Noeline, you're coming with me in my car. We must leave now so we get to the church before the bridal party."

But now my umbrella and raincoat were on the other side of the bride in her wide skirts, standing in the centre of the room. My pretty niece, smiling serenely, was ready for her own departure, her lace layers and train arranged for forward movement, and I would have had to ask her to move sideways so I could retrieve my rain gear. Well, I reasoned, it appeared that God had indeed answered the prayers of the Pentecostalists, so I decided I'd leave my coat and umbrella there and hope God continued to honour their petitions. As I went out to the stairs down to the main door, I murmured my situation to John, who laughed and told me he'd pray for continuing sunshine. At the foot of the stairs, an honour guard lined the hall: the senior residents of the home, some in wheelchairs, all with faces alight with excitement, were waiting to see the bride.

As we set off for the church, Yvonne picked up two elderly women who lived nearby, and then told us all, "We're running late. Everyone pray that we have green lights all the way to the church!" The other passengers dropped their heads in incessant murmuring prayers, with frequent and ecstatic hissings of "Lord Jeesuss." The first light was green. "Green light! Hallelujah!" shouted Yvonne, putting her foot down hard on the accelerator. "Everyone pray for the next one!" For myself, I was praying that I would be able to cope with the service in a Pentecostalist church, and the Pentecostalists themselves. These people are not your enemies, I kept telling myself over and over; they are churchgoers like yourself. The murmured prayers were interrupted by lifted heads and cries of "Hallelujah!" as all the traffic lights along the Staines High Street turned out to be green. "The Lord has heard our prayers! Hallelujah!" bellowed Yvonne, as she rounded a corner off the end of the street so fast we passengers had to clutch our seats, and then pulled up in the parking lot with a squawk from the hand brake.

We entered the low, white church where a piano was playing softly and the pews were mostly full. As the aunt of the bride, I was ushered to a pew near the front and was just in time to make another quick prayer for survival before the pastor – Pastor Paul, I'd been told – brought the handsome, smiling bridegroom, Lee, and his brother, the best man, to the front. Yvonne was turning around in her seat to various attendees and I knew she was affirming that the Lord had heard their prayers. My sister Margaret came up the aisle with an usher and was shown to her seat of honour in the pew ahead of mine. The pianist struck up the wedding march, and the wedding party entered, first Jeanne-Marie, as bridesmaid, and then Kim, on her father's arm, smilingly swayed up the aisle to join Lee in front of the beaming Pastor Paul.

The marriage service began. We sang hymns that were like songs, the congregation swaying to the rhythm as they sang, and often calling out "Hallelujah!" along with more hissed, ecstatic murmurs of "Lord Jeesusss." They were silent during the exchange of vows, with an eruption of hallelujahs after Pastor Paul pronounced them man and wife. He then had the wedding party sit, and said, "At the bride and groom's request, I am to make a plea that all present who have not accepted the Lord Jesus Christ as their own personal saviour will do so now."

This was what I had been hoping wouldn't happen, bringing up the terrible fear that gripped me when I had attended such services as a teenager. Pastor Paul launched into his evangelistic message, his previously genial tone now hectoring and threatening, his smiling face now stern, punctuated by shouts of "Hallelujah!" and accompanied by near-orgasmic murmurs of "Lord Jeesuss" as the congregation swayed in ecstasy. I clenched my handbag with both hands as the once-familiar, fear-filled, roaring darkness began to surround me. "Oh God," I prayed in desperation, "please help me."

At that moment, the high windows flashed with bright light, immediately followed by such a violent clap of thunder it seemed the low roof would fall down upon us. Then the windows went black as rain drummed on the roof so loudly Pastor Paul had to raise his voice to a shout. But his exhortations were lost to me in the elemental din, even the hallelujahs from the congregation barely audible above the sound of the downpour.

Somehow, above the tumult, we recognized the signal for the last hymn, and then the wedding service was over. Pastor Paul led the wedding party to the vestry to sign the register, and the rest of us crowded into the narrow aisle and small porch to wait for our cars. And I now saw that those faithful Pentecostalists, who had prayed for and received sunshine, and had thanked the Lord for it, were shrugging their bodies into raincoats, the women pulling out and unpleating transparent plastic rainhats they had stowed in their handbags, and both men and women fetching umbrellas from a holder in the porch. As we shuffled forward, frequent cries went up. "Everyone for so-and-so's car!" and, frantically opening their umbrellas, the passengers scuttled down the steps in the rain to the waiting cars. On the porch, I found myself beside John again. "Look at me," I wailed. "I believed their prayers had been answered. I'm only in my dress and all of them brought their raincoats and umbrellas!"

"Oh they of little faith," he laughed. At that moment, the call came for me. "Yvonne's car! Everyone who's going with Yvonne!"

I stepped forward, fearing for my dress and hair, let alone my suede handbag, resigned to all becoming drenched and my dress and bag ruined, my chignon collapsed. But just as I moved from the shelter of the porch, an invisible hand swept aside the curtain of rain and clouds; the sky was suddenly blue, the sun shining brightly from it as I sashayed down the steps, menaced by nothing but a few raindrops falling from the eaves. My hair, dress, and bag dry, I got into the car beside Yvonne for the short drive to the wedding reception.

As she jammed her foot on the accelerator and we rocketed off, Yvonne called, "The Lord heard our prayers! The sun has shone for the bride! Hallelujah!"

## 2. Night Bus to Amsterdam

The clerk in Dover studied my ticket and passport. "Where's your visa for France?"

"What visa?"

"You have a Canadian passport. You need a visa to travel to France."

She was misunderstanding my situation. I said, "But I'm not staying in France. I'm going right through to Amsterdam."

"You still need a visa to travel through France."

I was patient with her. "I'm boarding the bus on the ferry. It's going nonstop to Amsterdam."

"It doesn't matter. You still need a visa to travel through France." She hadn't misunderstood.

I resorted to the classic and useless question of the thwarted. "But how do I get a visa? No one mentioned it before. What am I to do?"

The clerk shrugged. "You could go back to London and get one. Your travel agent in London should have told you. You could phone them and ask them what you should do. The phones are over there." She was looking past me to the rest of the people in line.

I lugged my two bags over to the row of phones and thumped them against the wall. I had a hotel booking in Amsterdam for that night, and couldn't remember how to use a pay phone. As I tried to take a deep breath and tried to think, I heard a man with a Canadian accent talking on one of the phones. He was a big, dark-haired man with something familiar about the prominent black eyebrows and mustache. Beside him huddled an older, shorter, thinner man, all sandy-brown from his thin hair to his shoes, listening with a worried expression. I heard the man on the phone say, "To repeat: I have a Canadian passport and don't have a visa for France. My companion has a British passport and can go through France. We need to get to Amsterdam and don't want to go back to London for my visa. Is there something else we can do?"

He was in my situation. I eavesdropped as he listened; then he said, "Uh-huh" a couple of times, followed by "Right. Thanks. We'll run." As he replaced the receiver, I spoke up: "Pardon me for listening, but I have a Canadian passport and seem to be in the same position as you. No visa, and I need to get to Amsterdam too."

Picking up a suitcase, he said, "They told me there's a hydrofoil leaving for Belgium in 15 minutes. If we run, we can make it. Follow me!" He started to run, and, looking back over his shoulder, shouted: "We don't need a visa for Belgium! By the way, I'm Frank and he's Ronnie!"

Ronnie looked at me in a worried way; then he picked up the larger of my bags and their other suitcase, and began running after Frank. I gathered up my smaller one and followed. Frank was running fast, in a practised and graceful way; Ronnie, older and obviously less fit, ran just ahead of me, looking back to see if I was keeping up. We followed Frank through a maze of concrete tunnels; I was just glad that he seemed to know where he was going, and could tell the hydrofoil people that two others were behind him. We panted up behind him as he turned and said, "The weather's bad and the hydrofoil isn't leaving. But there's a ferry, back where we came from. Run!"

Off he went again, back through what may or may not have been the same maze of concrete tunnels. But we were too late. Frank had just discovered that the ferry had already departed. We slumped onto one of the wooden benches lining the middle of a big room, I a little apart from them, not wanting to intrude. Frank and Ronnie began discussing what they should do, Frank's resonant voice clearly audible and Ronnie's face even more worried. This had been their last hope. It was useless – they'd never get to Amsterdam now – they'd better return to London. Perhaps they should settle for a holiday in London after all. They had better phone Hans, but he'd just had the flu, he may be sleeping, they wouldn't want to wake him up.

It was Thursday, I had a hotel room in Amsterdam booked for that night through Monday, and I was leaving from Schiphol airport on Tuesday to return home to Edmonton. I looked around the room. One wall was lined with the booths of ticketing clerks, all with nothing to do. Leaving my luggage beside the bench, I went to one of the wickets and explained my situation to the agent.

No problem, the agent promptly said, provided you can wait for a few hours. A bus for Amsterdam's leaving London at 8 p.m., connecting with the ferry to Ostend at 10 and arriving in Amsterdam at

7 a.m. tomorrow. There're plenty of seats left. Because it's going through Belgium, you won't need a visa. Much relieved that I would arrive in Amsterdam, although some hours later than I'd intended, I bought a ticket..

Waving my ticket, I returned to Frank and Ronnie, and told them. It was as if I'd come up with something quite extraordinary; they listened, galvanized, their expressions transformed from despair to euphoria. "How clever you are!" cried Frank. "Ronnie, we'll buy tickets right now!" He tore over to the clerk as if he feared a sudden rush of people in the door taking up the remaining seats. Returning with their tickets, he beamed at me. "You've saved our holiday!"

I was now part of Frank and Ronnie's holiday. With hours to fill, we stowed our luggage in the lockers that lined one wall of the room, and walked out to see Dover. Frank pointed to a Marks and Spencer. "I must buy some Double Devon toffees! Ronnie recommended them to me and now they're my favourites." We each bought a bag of Double Devon toffees and went back out into the street munching.

When the shops began to close, Frank told me they would be buying my dinner. "We insist. You saved our holiday," he said. Dinner was what they considered the best fish and chips chain in England. Seated opposite me as we waited for our orders, they told me about themselves; rather, Frank did. He was an actor. He had been a stand-in for Burt Reynolds – that explained the familiar look – and pointed to his black leather jacket. "Burt gave this jacket to me," he said. He opened it. "See?" On the gold silky lining, embroidered in cursive writing on two lines, I read "To Frank, Love from Burt." I looked suitably impressed. Under the jacket he was wearing a finely-knitted sweater, in ivory silk. A knitter myself, I exclaimed over it. Frank beamed. "Isn't it lovely? Ronnie sent it to me for my birthday two years ago. It's my favourite sweater."

Ronnie, he told me was a real English butler, butler to a duke. Ronnie merely smiled. Trying to imagine him as a Jeeves or Bunter, and wanting to draw him into the conversation, I said, "Gosh – which duke?" Ronnie then named a duke whose name I recognized as being one of the richest men in England. He added modestly, "I'm only his office butler, in London. I arrange his dinner parties and so on. He has another butler in the country." This was at the time when speculation regarding the marriage of the Prince and Princess of Wales, Charles and Diana, was at its height. "So," I surmised, "you arrange dinner parties when royalty is there too?" Ronnie acknowledged that this was part of his duties; he arranged the seating at the tables. I looked at him expectantly, but he continued to smile serenely at me, the tactful English butler.

Frank went on to tell me that they stayed with Hans every year. Hans had a house right on one of the old Amsterdam canals, tall and modern, all glass. He told me where I could stand, on the other side of the canal, to see it. "You must go there and look over at it. You can't miss it."

Needing my turn, I told them I would be staying in a small hotel on the Prinsengracht, and that this time I was looking forward to visiting the Van Gogh Museum, which had opened since I was last there. "I've never been to any of the museums," Frank said. "I'm out in the bars all night so I'm never awake when the museums are open." Turning to Ronnie, he said, "We really should get to them this time."

After our fish and chips and cups of tea, we had run out of things to say to each other so we returned to the ferry office with more than two hours to spare. Ronnie and I read while Frank napped, until, at last, it was announced that the bus from London, en route to Amsterdam, had now arrived and passengers were to line up to board and take their seats. We retrieved our bags and filed out of the door at the end of the room into a dark tunnel to check our luggage and claim our seats on the tall, brightly lit bus. When we were all aboard, I in one of the window seats near the front, Frank and Ronnie somewhere behind me, the bus drove the short distance onto the ferry, where we all had to get off again for the trip across the Channel.

Frank and Ronnie ushered me up companionways to a huge passenger cabin, lined with booths, consisting of banquettes in pairs, separated by a table. We ensconced ourselves in one and Frank rushed up to the bar. He came back with triple single-malts for us all. Putting my scotch on the table, I stretched my legs out on my banquette and opened my book. Frank was agog to go over the ferry and wanted Ronnie to go with him. "No," said Ronnie, remaining seated opposite me. "You go. I'm staying here to rest with Noeline."

"Are you sure?" asked Frank, looking almost worried in his turn. Ronnie hoisted his legs up onto his banquette. "Off you go, Frank. Enjoy yourself." Drink in hand, Frank rushed away.

Ronnie and I, stretching out each side of the table, exchanged a look and smile that meant we both wanted to rest quietly, without further talk. We alternately read and napped, sipping our drinks from time to time. We were interrupted by two exuberant visits from Frank: "Oh Ronnie, I've met the sweetest Irish boys. We're having such a party out on the deck! Are you sure you won't come?" and then, "Oh Ronnie, those Irish boys are killing me, they're so funny! I'm having a wonderful time!" Each time Ronnie smiled and murmured, "I'm glad, Frank."

Last call brought him back to buy us all another round of triple single-malts, just before the announcement that everyone must return to their vehicles. "Drink up!" Frank urged. "We deserve it!" Groggy with Scotch and interrupted naps, I drank some more, and then followed Frank and Ronnie down into the bowels of the ship to our bus, Ronnie making sure I was just behind them. On the bus, we took our same seats. Soon the bus was driving off the ferry and running down a very wide, wet, black freeway, rain shining in the bright, multiple lamps on each side.

Sleep and several ounces of Scotch were beginning to catch up with me when I heard shouting behind me. Turning round, I saw Frank standing on the short flight of steps which led down to the lavatories. He was addressing some young men sitting in the back of the bus: "So you wanna come down with me and see me drop my pants and pee – is that what you want?"

I looked for Ronnie on their seat and saw him in a sandy huddle against the window, staring ahead. The boys were shouting back, and one of them rushed forward, fists up, as Frank bellowed, "So I'm gay! That bothers you, asshole?"

At that fraught moment, I realized that the bus was crossing the many lanes of the freeway and slowing down. As it pulled up on the shoulder, Frank froze at the top of the steps as did the boy in the aisle. The driver slowly unfolded himself from his seat. He was huge. He padded down the aisle, swaying from foot to foot like a bear. He loomed above the combatants, and said in Dutch-accented English, "If you don't all shut up right now, I shall throw the lot of you off the bus."

The boy who'd made the rush up the aisle slunk back to his seat and Frank disappeared down the steps. In total silence, the driver returned to his seat and pulled the bus back onto the freeway and across the lanes again. I went to sleep, waking briefly once to look back at Frank and Ronnie. They were both fast asleep, Ronnie's sandy head on Frank's black leather shoulder, Frank's black moustache on top of Ronnie's head.

69

I woke up for good when the bus pulled up beside a café. It was 5 a.m., somewhere in the southern Dutch countryside. The night was still black but it was no longer raining, and the white glare of the café promised coffee and Dutch bread rolls. Looking back, I saw Frank and Ronnie still asleep, Ronnie's head now resting against the window, Frank curled up facing the aisle. They were still in the same position when I returned to the bus.

They woke as the bus pulled into Amsterdam station, and, still yawning, joined me as I was claiming my bags. Ronnie hailed a taxi for me, and they both carried my bags to the driver. When I thanked them, Ronnie smiled tiredly and Frank said, "It's nothing. You saved our holiday!"

### 3. Bomb Scare Flight

My flight from Schiphol airport home to Edmonton began uneventfully. The Canadian Airlines plane left on time, at 1:30 p.m. on a clear, mild January afternoon, for the eight hours' flight to Edmonton, due to arrive at the local time of 3:30 p.m.

The plane was full, and although I was in the centre row, at least I had an aisle seat. Struggling with my mild claustrophobia on crowded planes, I looked at the young man in the seat next to me, hoping he would be conversational and take my mind off it. But he returned my tentative smile with the haughtiest of glances before raising a thick academic-looking book so far up to his face it was almost scraping his glasses, blocking me out of his line of vision. So I took out my book, a decidedly less academic one, and held it up to my own face.

The flight was about an hour old when the strange announcements began. "Would the passenger who wishes to exchange his seat please come forward to the cockpit and identify himself?" Now settled into my book, I thought this sounded odd, but only momentarily.

A short time later, the captain repeated the message: "Would the passenger wishing to change his seat please come forward to the cockpit?" Over the next few hours, the announcement was repeated; it was almost getting irritating. Surely, I thought, a simple seat exchange would be handled by the cabin attendants.

But over those hours, the flight continued as usual. The plane proceeded along its steady path through the skies, its white noise of dull roar overlaid with whine unvarying. The drinks and food carts rattled as

70

cabin attendants pushed and pulled them up and down the aisles. The passengers read, dozed, ate and drank, chatted to seat mates, got up to go to the lavatories and returned to their seats.

As we came toward the end of our allotted eight hours of flight, and the cabin attendants were moving back and forth collecting the leftover tumblers and food trays, the next announcement was different in tone. "By now, all passengers will be aware that we have a problem passenger on board." Was I aware of this? A passenger wishing to change his seat was a problem passenger? Was it some sort of code for something worse?

The dispassionate voice went on, "We will not be landing in Edmonton until the airport is cleared of all other planes and security arrangements are in place. We estimate that our landing in Edmonton will be delayed by at least one hour. We will let you know when we are to land as soon as we hear from the ground."

It must indeed be something worse. I thought of a bomb or highjackers. The young academic forgot to disdain me: his book now down on his lap, eyes alive with excitement behind his glasses, he turned to me and hissed, "I think it must be a bomb!"

Gratified to able to put him in his place, I put on my best eyes-blazing manner as I hissed back, "Shut up! You can't use that word on a plane!" He turned his face back to his book, as did I while I thought about what I would do if we were being highjacked – bullets may start flying. Across the aisle was a young mother with a small child in the seat next to her and a baby on her lap. She would need help; I could dive over to her seat and grab a child. A bomb, I couldn't conceive of: I saw our enemy as human, the problem passenger of the announcements.

The ordinariness within the cabin was almost eerie. No one exclaimed, screamed, or went into hysterics. The engines continued to roar, the passengers continued doing what they had been doing, the attendants calmly traversed the aisles. It was as if the captain had made only a routine announcement regarding our descent into Edmonton for our scheduled arrival time.

Finally, the captain announced that we would now be making our descent into Edmonton. "All passengers are to remain in their seats, their seatbelts fastened, until told what to do."

The plane descended into the pale orange light of a late prairie winter afternoon, skimming above the blue, snow-covered landscape. I heard the grind of the landing gear descending below me, and then our plane touched down with a small, reassuring bump on the runway. Nothing had happened in the air; we were safe; we were on home ground.

While the plane roared over the tarmac toward the distant airport buildings, the captain reminded us to stay in our seats until further instructed. When the main building drew near, I was struck by the unusual emptiness of the tarmac: no other planes were in sight, and there was none of the usual activity of vehicles moving about with flashing lights, personnel standing by the gates. Our solitariness was cemented by our coming to a stop well out on the apron, away from the buildings. As the engines whined down into silence, we were again reminded to remain in our seats. I wondered what my husband would be thinking, waiting for me in the airport, and whether he knew what was happening.

Then there was a thump as steps were positioned outside the front door of the aircraft. The captain told us that we would now be leaving the plane, but we must take only our coats with us, leaving everything else at our seats. As I stood up, put on my coat and gloves, and lined up in the aisle, I thought how strange it was to leave my possessions at my seat, even my book and handbag.

One by one we walked out the door into the frigid air and down the steps. Now I saw that we were not alone after all: the plane was ringed by kneeling and standing men dressed in camouflage, guns at their shoulders pointed toward us and the plane.

The cabin attendants guided us over the apron to the building, and then through an unaccustomed door over to one side. Inside, we were ushered into a large room, where we were again told to wait for further instructions. Several passengers rushed to a row of pay phones, and I realized that I had interpreted the instructions so literally I hadn't even thought to take coins from my handbag to make a phone call.

A long table at the front of the room bore urns of coffee and stacks of packaged sandwiches, and we were told to help ourselves without charge. These were welcome because we were to spend the next four hours in that room. I found myself sitting beside a woman lawyer in Edmonton. Normally, I would have asked her why she had gone to Amsterdam, what she saw, and where she stayed. But we talked only of our work and lives in Edmonton. I asked her if she watched *LA Law* on television, which a lawyer friend of ours despised; she said she enjoyed it, hating to miss an episode. We exchanged business cards.

Not only did our conversation help the long hours pass, but assured me that beyond that room, and the airport itself, everyday life was waiting.

From time to time we were summoned into lines. We were fingerprinted. We were asked to submit a sample of our handwriting. We were questioned: "Did you see anything suspicious? Did you see any passenger behaving in any way you would consider at all abnormal?" These indignities angered some passengers. "Fingerprinting me, as if I was a common criminal!" "What do they mean, did I see anything suspicious? How would I know?"

Having almost cut my teeth on the thrillers my mother loved, I happily cooperated, wishing I had seen something suspicious so I could help, and rather intrigued at being fingerprinted for the first time. After each of these episodes, we returned to our seats to resume our wait. I asked my companion if, as a lawyer, she had any objections to being fingerprinted and questioned. She laughed, "Not at all. They have a job to do. I wish I could have helped more, but I didn't see a thing." Her matter-of-fact reply put the crisis, whatever it was, in its place as an abnormal happening that was now over, at least for us. Our hours in the room were to come to an end, and we would be released to our everyday lives.

This was soon confirmed when announcements were made that passengers with ongoing connections and those with small children were to line up at the outside door to be escorted to the plane to retrieve their possessions. Airport life outside our room must be returning to normal. We watched as police officers led them off, in pairs or small family groups, through the door and outside, not to return.

But my anticipation of release to normality was now hampered by a small but vexing problem that had been nibbling at the edges of my mind, preventing me from merely feeling impatient to be gone from the airport. In Schiphol, I had misinterpreted the duty-free regulations for alcohol, and had bought a bottle each of Scotch and cognac instead of the one allowed me. This loomed over me as a hurdle that I knew would tax all my remaining energy when I was to be finally released, in spite of telling myself that the worst that awaited me was receiving a reprimand and having to pay some amount of duty.

Finally, those of us with neither ongoing connections nor accompanying children were told to line up at the door to be escorted back to the aircraft. In twos also, we were accompanied by a police officer as we made our way through the cold darkness back to the plane. That done, we were taken back to the building, but to another room, to line up for customs and immigration. We filled that room with our several long lines.

Suddenly, our collective calm was broken. Another flight had arrived, its passengers crowding the back of the room. We of the Canadian Airlines flight from Amsterdam were all ordered out of our lines and back to the walls while they took our places in the lines down the room. As one, we all shouted: "Why them? Why not us!"

After all the other passengers had at last gone through the doors, we were told to form our lines again. I now felt very tired, and my customs error loomed large. I would hold up the others in line behind me, I would be detained and questioned further, I would have to fill out forms, I would have to pay money, I would have to wait while the receipt was filled out and issued to me, and all this before I could collect my luggage, meet my husband, and go home. I stepped out a little from my line and gazed ahead to get a look at the official surveying the customs forms at the top of my line. I had chosen the wrong line: this was an unsmiling young man, who stared sternly out from behind his glasses at each individual. He was not going to be nice.

At last it was my turn. I stepped forward and handed the young man my form. He gave me the same stern gaze before his eyes dropped to my form, and back up again at me.

"You have something to declare?" he asked me, again with that stare. I fought down a sigh, and explained – I had misread the instructions in Schiphol and bought one more bottle of liquor than was permitted, a bottle of cognac and a bottle of Scotch.

The totally unexpected happened. The man's face, which had been staring at me fixedly and humourlessly, now broke into a smile. It was a sweet smile: his lips curled up at the corners, and even the corners of his eyes crinkled. "I think," he said, his voice now gentle, "that that's the last thing we'll be worrying about tonight." Taking up a pen, he wrote a big red "OK" across that part of my form. But he didn't let me go without an admonition: "When you get home, pour a stiff drink from one of your bottles and get a good sleep. You've earned it."

Beyond was yet another room into which I stumbled, more with relief than fatigue, to see my suitcase in duplicate, its physical bulk standing before me and its insides on a screen to one side, being scrutinized by yet another official. "That's just fine," he said as he handed my case to me, and I almost ran out through the double doors to my waiting husband. As we made our way through the airport and out to the car, the freezing air felt caressingly soft, almost tropical. I was safe; after a short car ride, I would be home.

**Coda**: We discovered later that handwritten messages had been distributed and found by the crew in various parts of the plane, stating that there was a bomb on board which would be detonated unless the plane bypassed Edmonton and went on to Vancouver. The combined efforts of Dutch and Canadian police never succeeded in locating the writer of those threatening messages.

*Trapeze, David Skyrie, 2011*

# Edward Lemond

## Kathy

Kathy was the girl for me. She was quick, funny, bright, and very pretty. There were other girls I liked and other girls who liked me more than Kathy did, but it was Kathy, or the thought of Kathy, that was lodged in my brain, deeper than sin. So strong was my attraction to her that I could not stay away for long but always wanted to be going where I would be most likely to find her. Every Sunday I attended youth group at church because I knew she'd be there, one Sunday I asked her if she wanted to play a round of miniature golf on the way home, she could not think of any reason to say no, the next Sunday I asked her again, she liked going places and doing things, nothing serious, fun, that was her favorite word, fun, one Sunday we went to a movie, when I tried to put my arm around her shoulders she said, We agreed we wouldn't do that, I wasn't sure what the *that* was that we had agreed not to do, the drive home was like a dream, everything familiar yet strange at the same time, so strange that I could not have said with any assurance, yes, this is the river that runs through the town where I live, yes, this is the church I go to, yes, this is the school I attend, yes, this is the A & W where I hang out with my friends, the porch light was on, Mike, her brother, was inside the house watching TV, I could not think of anything to say, Mike knocked on the window, she did not come to church the next Sunday, she did not attend youth group, Don't ask me, Mike said, Is she sick, She's decided to switch churches, Why, She doesn't want to see you anymore, See me, Look we still have the rest of the summer, we can still do the things we said we wanted to do, a small hard bubble of fury broke in the middle of all that pain, I told him maybe I didn't want to spend so much time with him, maybe I was sick of hanging around with him doing the same old things, maybe there were more important things in life than driving around the back roads all night long and never getting laid, with his dark hair, dark eyebrows and square jaw Mike did not look at all like Kathy, I sometimes thought that they must have different fathers, That's your choice, he said, I told him I had already made my choice and as far as I was concerned he could go to hell, the rest of the summer I kept to myself, avoiding all those places where I might run into Mike and the gang that Mike was part of, I stayed at home, reading, listening to the radio, practicing my instrument, refining my fingering, one evening toward the end of August I went to the field for a run, I hadn't seen him in weeks, I felt shy, he felt shy, afraid that some word, some gesture, might spark the old animosity, we ran a few laps together, I seemed to be able to breathe for the first time in weeks, we said how much we missed each other, summer gave way to autumn, the outer world seemed to mirror the inner, the football team won more games than it lost, one Sunday in October we drove to a place we knew, a creek where there was swimming hole under a bridge, a hundred yards from the swimming hole, where the banks were smooth and muddy and slippery as a pole covered in pig fat, we played a game we'd played a hundred times in different settings, different seasons, where the boy who could push the other one down the mud bank into the water was King of the Castle, at first it was horse play, slipping, sliding, laughing, leaping, we covered ourselves in mud, then more serious, pushing, pulling, kicking, rolling, fighting to gain the advantage, because of his powerful build, his strong arms, his lower center of gravity Mike gained the upper hand, I rested below in the water, gathering my strength, biding my time, waiting for him to come to me so I could wrap my arms around his ankles and pull him down, down into the water, face down in the water, face down in the water, I was holding him down in the water, down in the water, holding his head down in the water while he swung with his powerful arms, left and right, down in the water, down in the water, until I let go, swam away, toward the other shore, on my back, fighting to catch my breath.

Days went by, weeks. Mike was changing. With his dark features, square jaw, and infectious smile, friends were telling him he ought to get into the movies. He was a popular figure at school. Girls stopped and talked with him in the hallway. Arriving at school or leaving he was always surrounded by a dozen other boys all dressed alike, in yellow cords, all very animated. Very rarely did I see Kathy, then only from a distance. She was active in several different groups at school, including Future Teachers, A Cappella Choir, and Sun Shiners. When she wasn't busy with some activity or other, she was always at a friend's house. I began to attend church regularly, the same church that Kathy attended because I knew I would see her there. She sang in the choir. She was involved in acolyting and confirmation. She attended youth group. One Sunday I waited for her on the steps of the church, I said the only thing that was on my mind, the only thing I had been thinking about for weeks, for months, Why don't you want to see me anymore, she glanced around, at the church above, at the street below, where a car might arrive at any moment to whisk her away, Would it be okay if I drove you home after youth group, No, it wouldn't, close up the freckles on her face seemed to be in the shape of little five-pointed stars, I wondered if this was a new kind of makeup, Every time I want to talk to you you're too busy, a car pulled up by the curb, Mike opened the door, Kathy had dated other boys before but never any one boy for any length of time, but now, as if to drive one more nail into my coffin, she made it known that she was going out with a new boy, with a name like a girl's, Alison, in the scheme of things Al as he preferred to be called and who wouldn't was a nobody, a poor student, a failed athlete, an outsider, in short he had no status, I wondered what Kathy saw in him, I followed her wherever she went, I went to church every Sunday and helped with the collection because I knew she'd be there, I attended youth group for the same reason, even when it became clear that Al had suddenly got religion too, I stood in the door at school where I knew she'd come in after whispering one last sweet nothing into his ear, I circled the streets and alleyways near her house, sometimes I'd drive right in front of the house, gunning the motor, not looking, then come around the block and do it again, I'd park the car a few houses away under a tree and sit there and watch her, them, without her, them, being able to see me.

Winter passed, and then it was spring. The evening of Good Friday youth group were re-enacting the Stations of the Cross. The audience was small but attentive, mostly family members. No one was leaving, even as the end neared. I was standing in the door of the vestry, behind the choir stalls, looking out. In the Fifth Station I had played Simon the Cyrene, who was taken from the crowd and ordered to carry the cross, when Jesus stumbled. In the Twelfth Station I had played the centurion who offered Jesus a cloth soaked in vinegar when He thirsted. Though I had no further part to play I wasn't bored. I was waiting for the end to come for I had chosen this evening, this occasion to speak to Kathy and find out her true intentions. I remembered the lie about Simon, that it was he and not Jesus who was nailed to the cross, I wished it were true, if only because it would have given me another part to play, the stone was in place, sealing the tomb, Kathy, as Mary Magdalene, came forward, all eyes were on her as she stopped before the sealed tomb to pray, Please God, she said, quite loudly so all could hear, Where doth the Lord dwell, the ensuing silence seemed to suggest that anything was possible, I scribbled a few words for her on the back of a program, when she came around the end of the choir stalls I don't think she even saw me until I handed her the program, thrust it in her face, it took her a second or two to glance at my note before shaping her lips into a big, fat, round no, standing backstage all evening, with nothing to do, had left me feeling primed for action and so with a sort of explosive and half-unconscious sense of myself I moved backwards into the frame of the door to block her route of escape, I guess she feared a scene, sighing she said she'd go with me on one condition, that I would never, ever do something like this again, I clapped my hand over my heart, as if to quiet that which would not be quieted, I swore I never would, we drove out of town, along Sixth Street to South, along South to River Road, along River Road toward a town called Lebanon, the car was taking a long time to warm up, Kathy was cold, it was getting dark, once we were outside town the darkness was more profound than any I could remember, the road curved down close to the river, the river was high because of the spring run-off but not so high as to flood the road as it sometimes did, I turned off the motor, Do you want to walk down to the river, I said, No, she said, I did not find it strange that she had never really wanted to go out with me, what seemed strange was that she had agreed to date me at all, we were so different in so many ways, she must have seen from the beginning that it was impossible even if I did not, she was the only girl I ever really wanted with my whole heart, she said there was something she wanted me to understand, she did not look at me when she talked, she looked at the dashboard or something just above the dashboard, the windshield wipers, she seemed to need something to look at to keep her thoughts in focus, Since I've met Al I've changed, she said, when I'm with Al it's like I know who I am, I don't have to put on an act, there's just him and me, sitting there, talking, I bet that's not all you do, I said, sit there and talk, We have to be sure we're doing the right thing, she said, the more she talked the more I realized I had no idea what she was talking about, she was not even talking to me but to some imaginary person standing on the road by the car, Listen, I have to ask you something, I said, my voice suddenly much deeper than I could ever remember, Can't you stop talking about Al for one minute, Christ Almighty you're obsessed, what do you want to do, get married and have a bunch of kids, what about all the things you wanted to do in life, remember, you wanted to be a teacher, you wanted to travel, what about all that, I can still teach, What about me, What about you, Where do I fit in, she looked at me for the first time all evening, she didn't laugh, didn't cry, didn't shout, just looked a little sad, a little depressed, I would not listen to what she was saying, I kept insisting on the impossible, I don't know what you're talking about, she said, I've got feelings too, you know, I said, she sat in the dark by the window looking down at her hands folded in her lap, I dared not utter another single syllable, through a crack in the window I could hear the river below, the water sloshing the bank, peepers in the shallows, I wanted to lock the door and never let them in, never let her out, I didn't even hate her, when she finally did speak again it was only to say that she was cold and wanted to go home, I started the car, I did not say another word, I think she was grateful for that.

# Nobody Here By That Name

I had signed up for the class in English romantic poets because I wanted to meet a girl. Before I could say Hazlitt I had narrowed my choice to four good-looking girls who all sat together in the front row, except one. I was especially attracted to a blond girl whose laugh was infectious and who was always waving at a friend, she had so many. When I caught her eye one day and when she seemed to blink at me and smile, I found myself repeating, half out loud, two lines from a poem by Blake: *The harvest shall flourish in wintry weather/ When two virginities meet together.* I knew for a fact that at a minimum I was bound to be half right, which was encouragement enough.

And so it was that I followed the stunning blond, Judy Stein by name, into the hallway at the buzzer and stopped her at the top of the stairs, only to learn, in no uncertain terms, that she could not go out with me, why, because she was not free, why, because she was pinned to a member of the football team. Not pinned under, no such vulgarity, but pinned to. I had expected some such nonsense, I reminded myself, as she turned and disappeared down the stairs, into the circle of admirers waiting for her there below.

What stayed with me was the false smile Judy had given me, before whirling and dancing away. For hours, no matter what I stuffed into my mouth, I could taste nothing but ashes. A simple no turned out to mean more than a simple no, unlike what I had been lead to believe. I decided, then and there, never again to trust what I read, just because it's written in a book or in a newspaper. I skipped choices two and three and settled without further ado on number four, whom I had been, until now, on the verge of discounting.

Her name was Dolores, and she had lovely big brown eyes, a narrow sad pale mouth, and a hunchback. Her left shoulder was much smaller than her right shoulder. Her shyness had the effect of making me feel less shy and hesitant, or less ashamed of being shy and hesitant, which I suppose amounts to pretty much the same thing.

For our first date we went to see a movie, "Darling" with Julie Christie. After the movie we repaired to my place, prepared a plate of bread and cheese, opened a bottle of wine, and settled down to listen to a new record I had just bought, featuring songs from the operetta *Mahagonny* by the German composer Kurt Weill. Soon, though, it began to snow quite heavily, and I began to doubt if we would ever be able to get back to the residence where Dolores, or Dolly as she liked to be called, lived, more than a dozen blocks away.

"You could always sleep here," I suggested. "If you want to."

"Let's wait awhile," Dolly said, looking at me with her brown eyes.

"Sure," I said, "that's the thing to do, wait awhile." In the meantime I prayed for the furies of hell to continue their assault on my tiny abode, and, if they wished, to re-double it.

I put on the record and went into kitchen for a bottle of wine. I placed the uncorked *flasche* on the floor, along with two glasses, while Dolly, sitting in an armchair, short plaid skirt pulled halfway up shapely thighs, watched me with brown eyes and Lotta Lenya sang the Alabama song. I filled the two glasses with wine and handed one to Dolly.

"To life," she said, and I echoed her words. Sitting on the floor with my back against the armchair, with my eyes closed and my mind afloat, I stroked the soft breast of her calf. *Auf nach Mahagonny! Die Luft ist kühl und frisch. Dort gibt es Pferd- und Weiberfleisch ...* On to Mahagonny! The air is cool and fresh. There we'll find horse- and female flesh.

The discontented of all the continents are on the move to Mahagonny, the golden city. From Alaska come Jim, Jake, Bill, and Joe, with money in their pockets. It's girls they want, nothing but girls. If Jenny is too expensive for the other men, not so for Jim. It's not sex that Jim's interested in, it's love. All except Jim and Jenny drift away. The music grows quiet. Jim and Jenny are alone for the first time. They want to get to know each other. How would you like me to be, Jenny asks. Just as you are, Jim says. Do you like my hair combed forward or combed back, Jenny asks. You could change that around, depending on the occasion, Jim says. But what about my underwear, Jenny asks. Do I wear underwear beneath my skirt, or do I go without? Without! Jim says. As you like, Jenny says. And what are your wishes, Jim asks. It is too soon to talk of them, Jenny says.

The wine and the music made us forget everything. As my fingers came round the curve of Dolly's knee and began the slow, inexorable climb along her thigh, over the hill and into the valley – there came a loud knocking that shook us. I sat up and looked around. Someone or something was hammering at the back door. We were rudely awakened. Things had been going so smoothly. *Was soll sie auch hier halten? Ein paar Schenken und ein Haufen von Stille.* What did they want here? A few little gifts and a moment of quiet, if you please.

I got up and went into the kitchen and opened the door. Someone was standing there in the dark, in the thick snow, in a black sheepskin hat. "Who is it!" I demanded, almost blind with rage.

"Me," came the insolent reply.

I recognized the voice of a fellow student, one who attended the same German class as myself, and who distinguished himself by the fact that he was almost always absent. His name was Snyder, or Schmitt, depending on his mood, and he too lived off campus and dreamed of having a girlfriend, an even more remote possibility in his case. He wrote poetry and was on the board of the campus literary magazine. Once in a blue moon we got together to share a beer at the Scarlet Inn, in the basement of the Student Union.

"What the fuck you doing out in this weather?"

"Walking. What does it look like?"

"You're insane."

"Anybody home?"

"Just me and Dolly."

"Dolly?"

"You know." I rolled my shoulder.

"Are you going to let me in, or what?"

"Jesus Christ." I found another wine glass in the cupboard and led the way back into the living room. Dolly knew our friend by the name of Max, so Max it was for the remainder of the night. We settled down to listen to the lively and bitter tunes of Kurt Weill, Dolly in her armchair, Max against the wall by the kitchen door smoking a joint and sipping wine, myself on the couch examining the cracks in the ceiling.

Things in the city of Mahagonny were going from bad to worse. Jim in particular was disappointed with the state of things, calling Mahagonny a "manure pile" where nothing ever happened. *Ach, mit eurem ganzen Mahagonny wird nie ein Mensch glücklich werden, weil zuviel Ruhe herrscht und zuviel Eintracht and weil's zuviel gibt, woran man sich halten kann.* Ah, even with your great Mahagonny a man can never be happy, because there's too much peace and there's too much harmony and because there's too much that one can hold on to.

We did not say anything to one another when the music was over. The tone arm made a clicking noise, hesitated a moment, then lifted up. "Shall we hear more of the same?" I said, sitting up. "Or maybe something else? Maybe some Dylan, or some Cohen?"

"Mach nix," Max said in a muffled voice, between puffs.

"What do you say?" I looked at Dolly.

"Sure," she said, shrugging her shoulders.

*Sure* she says but what the fuck does that mean? Does it mean more Kurt Weill, or does it mean Bob Dylan, or does it mean L. Cohen? Kneeling on one knee by the record player, weighing my options, taking my sweet time, I was jolted back to reality by a very loud knocking, this time at the front door. "Christ Almighty," I muttered, looking around. "Will it never end!"

The knocking continued louder and louder. Before I could get to the door, men with flashlights burst into the apartment shouting "Freeze!" and "Hands up!"

I put my arm in front of my eyes because I was blinded. "What the," I started to protest, but a hand took hold of the front of my shirt and gave it a twist.

"Just shut up!" The hand thrust me back into the middle of the room.

"Okay Mac, get in there!" A second man emerged from behind the first, brushed past me, and went forward to secure the remaining rooms. I could hear Max's wine glass slip from his grasp, fall to the floor and break. Dolly sat hunched over in the armchair with her arms wrapped around her legs.

"Turn around and put your hands on top of your head!" I was told. The same set of hands patted me up and down looking for god knows what – a concealed weapon?

"Nothing! Okay, get down!" The next thing I knew I was on the floor, face down, arms stretched out above my head.

"That the prick?" the second man asked, pointing his flashlight at me. Both men were dressed in street clothes, and the only way we knew they wielded any authority was the kind of language they used.

"He doesn't fit the pic," the first man answered.

"What about this piece of shit?" The second man forced Max down to the floor next to me and gave him a little slap on the back of the head with his hand, which was twice the size of a normal hand. Max did the wise thing and played dead.

The first man passed the second man a photograph, showing the culprit they were looking for. "Fuck," the first man said. "What do we do now?"

"Maybe they're hiding him," the second man said.

"Good thinking," the first man said.

"Okay, you jerks," the second man said. "Where's the fuckass?"

Neither Max, nor myself, nor Dolly knew what they were talking about. I raised my head an inch from the carpet but before I could say anything one of the men kicked me hard in the ribs. "I said, where's the cunt!"

"Don't know," I sputtered.

"Mac, what the fuck's the prick's name?"

"Lemme look." He turned the photograph over. "Crumb, it says here. Michael Crumb."

"Nobody here by that name," I said.

"Listen, shitface, shutup till I ask you."

"What do we do now?" the second man asked.

"Check under the bed, asshole," the first man said.

It took them five minutes to turn everything upside down, in a fruitless search. There was nothing to be found, and this made them even madder. They began to blame each other. "Those queers back at the office gave a bum steer," the man called Mac said.

"Try the head," the first man said.

"We're wasting our time," the second man said.

"I know what your problem is, don't shit me," the first man said.

"You can't shit shit," the second man said.

"If I'm shit then we both know what you are," the first man said.

"Fuck you," the second man said, and he picked up his flashlight and left.

"Okay you imbeciles," the first man said, addressing Max, Dolly, and me. "Feel fortunate ..." Wheeling, blabbering, the two men vanished through the same door they had entered.

No one said anything for a long time. Max rolled over and sat up, some distance away. Dolly buried her face between her knees. I drew my hands in under my head and lay still, as still as possible when one's whole body is shivering. I looked at Max, but he would not return my look.

Dolly broke the silence. "I want to go home," she said.

"It's not nice out there," is all I could think of to say.

"I'm going," she repeated, and she gathered up her coat and her bag and went to the door.

"I'll go with you," Max said, coming to life. He found his

sheepskin hat in a corner of the room where one of the men had kicked it.

"Suit yourself," Dolly said.

I stood at the door and watched them disappear into the falling snow. I wanted to shout something at them, in the way of a good-bye, but I could not find the words.

# Never Say Die

It is the tenth day of my search, and I am alone, the others having given up. But why should I? I might see an eye, or a toe, or the bristle of a hair that no one else can see. I am his father, and I have more reason to look, and more need to find what I am looking for.

I wade downstream, away from the bridge where he fell. The water is chest-deep and I can feel the tug of the tide as the creek empties. The body could be anywhere – at the bottom of the creek, or buried in a mud bank, or washed out to sea. It could be someplace today where it wasn't yesterday, because of the action of the tides.

The water is muddy, and I cannot see much below the surface. Even if I dropped down into the water I would see nothing. I feel what's around me, with my hands and with my feet. I move in a zigzag, to cover as much of the creek bed as I can. I study the mud banks as the water level drops.

At low tide these banks are twenty feet high – slick mounds of mud that are mostly brown, sometimes silvery in the sun, sometimes blue when the sky bends down. Everything gets buried here – limbs of trees, shopping carts, hubcaps, beer bottles, coffee cups, twisted bodies of seagulls, discarded dolls, with sometimes only a jagged edge, or a corner, or a broken wing exposed to the watchful eye.

I've searched the creek twice already. I've searched the brook that flows into the creek. I've walked the shoreline of the river into which this creek and others drain. I've ridden in a helicopter to where the river opens into the bay. Nowhere, nowhere, have I, or anyone, seen a trace of him. Not a shoe, not a shirt.

I'm coming to a second bridge, close to where the creek flows into the river. Why not let myself go, out into the river? Why not see where the current carries me, the way it carried my son? Why not, if possible, experience what he experienced? But it's very possible that he experienced nothing. It's very possible that he was knocked unconscious when the train hit him. At most he experienced a moment of panic then nothing.

A voice calls to me as I drift under the bridge. It is Sophie. She does not want me to be doing what I'm doing. Not today. It's a holiday, she says. Come home. But for me there can be no holiday, as long as his body is being bruised by the elements. Celebrate if you must, I say to her. But let me do what I have to do.

Sophie is Steve's girlfriend and she's pregnant with their first child. They were always an unlikely couple – he a fisherman like me, tall, six feet seven, dark-skinned, dark-haired, a man of few words, she a poet, a teacher, auburn-haired, bright-eyed, not much over five feet tall. They had not planned to have children. They had talked about having an abortion.

On the way home in the car Sophie tells me about the poem she's written. Everyday she writes another poem about Steve. It's what keeps her sane, she says. She writes about the accident – what happened, what he did and what he didn't do, what she did and what she didn't do. She blames herself, which is only natural. The last line is always, "I can't believe you're gone."

She writes in longhand in a small black hardback artist's sketchbook that fits into the pocket of her down-filled jacket so she can take it with her wherever she goes. But today, because it's Thanksgiving, she's written something different. She and Steve were together for ten years. "Every day was a gift," she says.

She opens the book. She wants to read the poem she's written. Please, no, I shake my head. I can't possibly listen now. I'm still in the water, feeling the pull of the tide.

Instead of taking the usual way home, I double back, go around the traffic circle and follow the highway to the railroad overpass where the accident took place. I stop the car under the bridge and get out. Because it's late in the day, and because it's Thanksgiving, there are very few cars on the road.

It's Sophie's turn to say no. She doesn't want to follow me up the embankment to the railroad tracks. "I don't know where he is," she says, "but he isn't here."

I come up through a tangle of bushes that I grab hold of whenever I feel I'm slipping. I've been in the water under the bridge, several times, but this is the first time I've been up on top of the tracks. It's about half the length of a football field from the bridge over the highway to the bridge over the creek. The bridge over the creek is much older than the bridge over the highway. Steel girders, painted green, are set on top of ancient stone blocks, the sort you see in nineteenth century schools or monasteries.

I walk on the blackened ties, down the middle of the tracks. I walk where my son walked.

They had two dogs, Dutch, a Portugese water dog, and Bella, a Border Collie. Every evening after supper they went walking, sometimes along the path by the river, sometimes in the park, sometimes along the railroad tracks near where they lived. But one evening a train, in Sophie's words, "appeared on the bridge," where the tracks cross over the creek. It was the passenger train from Halifax, and it was an hour late. It had never been an hour late, in their experience, even in heavy snow.

Dutch ran ahead, as if to greet a long-lost friend. Steve called for him to come back but he would not. He ran down the middle of the tracks toward the train. Steve ran after him but though he was a young man, tall and fit, a good runner, an athlete in high school, a champion high jumper, a basketball player, he could not outrun the dog.

Sophie called for him to come back, but he would not. As long as there was a chance he could save Dutch – keep him alive – he had to keep running after him.

The train hit him and sent him flying, as if catapulted, over the side of the bridge to the creek below.

The tide was high, and flowing out. By the time Sophie had stumbled and fallen, gotten up again and slid down the embankment to the edge of the creek he was gone. Firemen, arriving within minutes, tied themselves to ropes and waded in. A diver searched underwater.

Police kept people back, but downstream, on the banks of the creek, on several pedestrian bridges over the creek, and on the highway that ran alongside the creek, where people stopped and got out of their cars to see what was going on, a sort of festive air took hold. Someone said it was a moose, stuck in the mud. A couple of boys tried to get a chant going. Where's the moose, they clapped, where's the moose.

A photographer took pictures – enough to fill two pages of a special edition of the local newspaper that came out the next day. Sophie saved them for me to see.

The railing is as old as the bridge, and as decrepit. It's made of wood and some pieces are visibly rotting. Others have splintered and broken away.

The mud here has a dirty look to it, unlike downstream where it feels like it's been washed clean. Large, flat, sharp-edged rocks jut from the banks. There's just enough water in the system at low tide to support a family of ducks as they float by. If he had fallen at low tide, the water would not have carried my son away the way it did. He might have hurt himself in the fall – broken a bone, broken his neck. Perhaps his injuries would have proved fatal, but he'd be there, we'd know. From here to the hospital is less than a mile. He might have been saved.

Someone's approaching along the tracks. Footsteps on gravel. It is Sophie.

"Are you all right?" I ask. Because she is walleyed, when Sophie looks at you she's also looking someplace else. You never know if she's really looking at you. What's in that other eye that's caught your attention, I want to ask her. Did you hear what I said, or are you just pretending you did? But I don't want to be rude.

She's right. This is a cold, desolate place where nothing of interest will ever happen again. He is not here.

Sophie is writing something in her book. I walk back the way I came.

On the other side of the tracks there's an electrical sub-station I hadn't noticed on the way in. Wires feed up the hill to the campus of the only university in town. The creek bends around the sub-station, circles back and runs close to the highway for another mile, before branching and burrowing into a marsh.

Just beyond the sub-station, between the creek and the campus, is series of playing fields, suitable for baseball, football, or soccer. Sea gulls have begun settling here for the night.

The clouds over the hills beyond the marsh are a deep, mottled pink.

Sophie's prepared a meatless lasagna for supper. Instead of pasta she uses slices of eggplant. There's garlic bread and a green salad. She pours two glasses of red wine. "To the kindest man I've ever known," she says.

After supper she reads me her poem. "Homage to One Who Lived His Life," she calls it. Her voice, when she reads, is different from her everyday voice. It's higher pitched, almost like song.

> *He never wrote a poem or painted a picture*
> *but his life was a work of art.*
> *I can easily see him*
> *at his desk, firing off e-mails*
> *in the name of his beloved fisherman's union*
> *whenever he felt an injustice …*

I have trouble following her words. I stop listening and just admire the way she says them. She has one eye focused on the words, while the other eye, unable to be at rest, wanders. She's aware that I've stopped listening but continues reading another minute or so before putting the book down.

There's more but she can't go on. She tries to look at me but can't, through her flood of tears.

I can't think of anything to say except, "Thank you."

The phone rings. Her mother wants her to come to dinner. It's not too late, she says, for Sophie to join the rest of the family around the table. Everyone misses her.

"I'm here with Ken," Sophie says. "I'm keeping him company. Or he's keeping me company."

I take the dogs for a walk while she prepares the couch for me to sleep on.

I sleep, at best, fitfully. When I wake, I don't know where I am. It's dark. I'm not in my own house. Just above where I'm lying there's a window that's faintly illuminated.

I hear Sophie's voice, from upstairs. "Yes," she says. And again: "Yes."

I know what she's going to tell me even before she comes down the stairs. The body's been found. We're to come in to identify it.

We don't say anything in the car on the way down. Sophie drives because she knows the streets and the roads.

The morgue is in the basement of the City Hospital. We follow the trolley down a long, narrow, empty corridor, painted the same pale green as the girders underlying the bridge where he fell. How bizarre is that, I say to myself.

Two policemen meet us at the door into the morgue. Sophie decides to wait outside. "Do you mind?" she says to me. "I can't bear the thought of what I might see."

"Of course not." One of the policemen stays with Sophie, and the other comes inside with me.

The orderlies have moved the body, still strapped to the rescue board, onto a stainless steel table. One of them removes the straps while the other stands aside. Then they both leave the room. The doctor in charge, a young woman who's surely no more than twenty-five years old, cuts the sheet, folding it to the side as she goes, clip by clip. She wears clear, tight-fitting, plastic gloves.

"You can stand here," the policeman says to me. I move to the head of the table.

The body is covered in the brown mud of the creek bed where it was found. The arms are tucked close to the side of the body but other features cannot be seen.

The mud is clay-like – reddish-brown, heavy, malleable earth, kept moist with repeated spraying, that takes whatever shape the doctor gives it as she pulls it away.

She finds the nose first. She uses various small tools to scrape the mud from the nose, the lips, and the area around the eyes.

There's a split in the upper lip, and a thick crust of dried blood. Behind the split the teeth have been knocked out.

She soaks a cotton pad with rubbing alcohol, leans close to clean the lips and the nose and the sockets of the eyes. She works slowly, carefully.

The eye sockets are empty, the eyes having been eaten away by fish or by seawater or by the tiny organisms that live in the mud where he was stuck.

All I can think of to say is, "Thank God Sophie doesn't have to see this."

Other than the damage to the face, and the two broken arms, the rest of the body is intact. The mud has kept the birds from picking at it.

The policeman suggests that I leave now. The body will be cleaned and kept in a cold room a few days, until the autopsy.

"I hope this will give you some closure," he says to me on the way out.

"That's not a word in my vocabulary," I answer.

"Just give it time," he says. "Go easy on yourself."

What, is he some sort of expert in the grieving process? Is that why he's here? Is that his job, to give me comfort?

As for Sophie, she cannot speak. She looks at me with terror in her eyes. All I can do is nod. Yes, it's him. She turns and walks away.

We are silent in the car. It is a cool, cloudy day. It looks like rain.

I didn't think it would be like this. I thought I would feel something.

I make a pot of coffee, and we sit together in the living room. She does not want anything to eat. She sits curled up in the armchair.

I'm worried about the baby. The baby is all that's left of Steve. I'd like her to see that too.

"I called Steve the day he died," I say.

She makes no response.

"It was a rough, windy day. The men were already on the wharf, waiting. The rain was horizontal, which still scares me, after thirty-five years on the boat. I thought to myself, what if I don't come back. I have to say something before it's too late."

She looks at me, wanting me to stop.

"He said it didn't matter what I thought. The two of you had to do what was best for you. I said I was speaking not just for myself, because I wanted a grandchild, but for the unborn child who could not speak for himself. He was angry and hung up."

Sophie, with her head back, gives out a sort of wailing sound, but soft, like a sigh. "I tried to get him to tell me what was the matter. He was in such a foul mood. We all felt it. Dutch felt it. I think it's why he ran off the way he did."

"I said what I had to say. I feel even more strongly about it now."

"You think you know him, because he was your son, but you don't. It was Steve who didn't want to have the baby. Look at me! Don't look away! It was Steve who said it would be a crime to bring a baby into a world as screwed up as this one. It was Steve who couldn't stop talking about all the wars and the killings and the rapes. All the way back to Alexander the Great. All the way back to Troy – and nothing, nothing, nothing has changed. Just as well not to be born."

"It doesn't matter what Steve thought. He's dead. It's up to you, to make up your own mind."

"We talked about it, we agreed."

"I won't stop pushing this, you know."

"What do you want from me?"

"I want you to keep Steve alive in some way. There has to be a trace, a sign that he was here. Even the air, when it blows, leaves a trace on the water."

"Steve will always be here, in my heart. I don't need this baby."

"It would be cruel, to kill this last breath that Steve will ever take."

"I'll tell you this. If I have the baby, it's not going to be for you. It's not going to be for Steve. It's going to be for me. And for the baby."

Her words silence me.

The air that trembled once an instant is still.

"To undertake is to achieve
Be Undertaking blent
With fortitude of obstacle
And toward encouragement"
　　　　- Emily Dickinson

## Fortitude of Obstacle

For example when you come down the stairs
One step at a time, hesitantly, as you face
Obstacles both old and new – such as failing
Eyesight, chronic weakness in the legs, poor
Memory, including for example how many steps
Are there to the bottom, or a memory that's too
Vivid, such as the memory of the pain that sometimes
Shoots through your hip – as you continue on down
What is there for me to do but watch and wait.

In the end it's not the money that counts, nor the prizes
You've won, but the people you love, and the people
Who love you. It's having work you wake up to
Every day with an intense desire to get at it.
It's not even happiness you seek or pursue,
At least not directly, but to be among people
You know you can trust and depend on. It's to know
You have survived, you did what you had to do
To survive in the face of whatever life could throw
Your way, in the shape of an obstacle, a hurdle,
A puzzle, or a trauma. Even more than wisdom,
Even more than happiness, even more than to be lucky
In your choice of friends, it is fortitude that matters.

But don't forget that although much has been lost
Much has also been gained, such as no longer living
Every moment thinking what your duty might be,
What you must do, without fail, before you can rest,
And also there's the sense that you no longer have to impress
Anybody for any reason, you are who you are and it's time
To stop feeling bad about yourself or thinking you must

Find excuses for this or that shortcoming.
And the really great thing is that you begin to bring
Your various cravings and addictions under control,
And you begin to feel a closing of the gap between
What the body demands and what the mind wants.

It's like when you enter a church and the candles
Are flickering and they begin to go out one by one,
And you wonder just how dark is it going to get,
And the surprise is that in the dark everything
Has its own shape and its own feel and everything
Is alive with its own energy and everything
Exists in the moment or not at all. The dark
Is no longer an obstacle but an opening
Into a space or realm in which
You have no memory of growing old.

*Fortitude, Elaine Amyot, 2012*

# Beth McLaughlin

## The Fly Boys

Come to think of it, of all the times I've been back, I've never seen a bird in here. You know how birds play in wind currents off high buildings or above the wake of a boat.

Whatever made us think we could climb that ten storey rock wall – let me tell you the story and maybe you can tell me what drove us to it.

We were stationed in northern Maine at the air force base, so, of course, on our off-duty days, we'd be looking for a little excitement. Grand Falls was the nearest big town and we thought Canadian girls were pretty fine. So, over we came, one hot summer day. The park here is the only public place offering a bit of shade and the high school kids hung out around here. We were just a couple of years older.

See that spiffy tourist shop over there. Back then it was an old shack smelling of French fries. A faded sign sat over the door frame, well, it was probably nailed on too. It said "Nature's wonders – the Wells 'n Rocks – 10 cents. We thought that was a hoot – 10 cents, so in we went. Same thing as today – through the building to a set of stairs that zigzagged down the side of the gorge almost to the river bottom. It was hot in the sun but it was nice and cool in the trees. I remember Buddy saying, "Amazing how life manages to thrive here" meaning on the sides of the cliff. Pretty soon, we were taking the steps two and three at a time. You know where the rest areas and lookouts are, well, we were racing past each other at those spots.

I remember Buddy, I know, pretty dull name, made a big jump off the last eight or ten steps and landed out on the first ledge. I caught up with him and almost knocked him into this big empty well. He'd stopped just at the edge of it – one of nature's wonders – about thirty feet deep. One well was full of water. We realized that in spring, the water came up to where we were standing – halfway up the canyon. They really do look like wells, don't they? But I'm getting away from my story.

So we continued, a little more carefully now, climbing down to the river. There were jagged rocks, smooth flat ledges, rocks that were curved, molded and heaved into existence – caves and wells and some loose rocks, but hell, we were in good shape from basic training, only six months or so earlier.

The river was lower than it is today and there was what you might call a mighty rough sidewalk beside it. Above us were two towering walls, holding the daylight between them. We were in the shade.

"Let's go down around that bend," says Buddy.

I said something about there being a dam up behind us, a little apprehensive you know, like any fool should have been.

"Oh come on Johnny," he sort of laughed at me. "You don't think they're going to open the floodgates do you? The water's too low and besides, what about us ignorant tourists?" And he laughed again. Then he said, "Hey, maybe there's an old path, like an Indian trail, back up to the park. Let's go see."

So, off we went. After a minute, we were leaping from stone to rock, I was doing my best to jump as fast and as far as possible, or, I should say, as fast and as far as Buddy. He was like a goddamn rocky mountain goat. Did I mention he had grown up in Colorado? Anyway, besides us, there wasn't a sign of life at all. And pretty soon, we were around the bend. See below where the river churns roughly to the left. From here, you can't really see the rock wall which was hanging over us and opened into this bowl-like formation.

From down there, it looked high but a lot more benign than from up here. And it was sunny on this slope again. Anyway, I remember looking up and noticing that old car frame, trying to bury itself in the side of the hill. I remember thinking it was a loose-faced rock wall, probably 120 degrees, measuring it from the river – pretty goddamn steep.

Buddy looked up, then looked at me and grinned.

A cold feeling sort of hit me, from inside. I guess I should have listened then.

Instead, I looked steadily back at him and said, "I suppose that rock face is only a little hill to you Buddy."

"Yeah, and look, there's the park fence, right at the top."

I gazed up – I could hear the kids' cries from way up, just faintly.

Buddy looked up again, then turned and said, "Do you suppose we could climb out of here and meet us some girls up there Johnny?"

"Well hell," I said, "we can always turn around and come back down if the going gets rough."

"Right on Johnny – I'll lead the way – you just tell me if you want to back down," he kind of laughed at the way he'd put it, you know.

Buddy started scrambling up the side of the bowl, I was right behind him. The first quarter wasn't so bad. Then of course, it was getting hotter and hotter and steeper and steeper. I had to lean into the rocks, you know, for fear of losing my balance. Then, I looked down. My eyes bounced like a fast zoom lens – I got dizzy. I froze, closed my eyes for a second and held on for dear life. I got them open again and realized I was sweating, a cold sweat, sure not from the heat. I got my senses back and called to Buddy to slow down and wait for me. I started crawling up towards him. I was almost caught up to him when my right foot slipped. Jesus, I thought I was lost right then. I squeaked something out and Buddy turned and bent to offer me a hand. You're not going to like what I tell you next...because...he fell. What happened? Let me tell you the rest. He fell, he didn't make a sound...and I didn't hear a thing for hours. I was paralyzed, my muscles were frozen stiff, my brain wasn't functioning, I couldn't look down, I couldn't look up – I don't remember seeing anything. Finally, this kid's voice penetrated my ear – I gradually figured out it was coming from over there, see where the park descends and goes around the edge of the bowl. I slowly moved my head. He was yelling, "need help"? and then something in French. One real smart one called out, "are you a fly boy, are you from Loring?" I nodded, I couldn't talk.

What seemed like another eternity passed. Then, I heard a chopper overhead – I was thrilled for a second, but then I realized I was too scared to let one finger off the grip I had and that I'd never be able to climb into a helicopter. Anyway, the chopper circled and hovered and landed on the ball diamond, then took off. But it couldn't get down inside this bowl – too small an opening. I learned later that it tried to come up the river between the walls but the gorge just wasn't wide enough.

I could hear kids' voices just above me now – above the old car frame clinging to the side of the cliff just like I was.

Then I heard another motor in the distance. A boat, I could hear the kids saying, going to get the other one.

A man's voice, very calm I remember thinking, called to me from the same old spot, it was the only spot I could be seen from, I realize now. "We're going to lower you a rope, from above that old car, do you know where the car is?" he called. I nodded again. "Do you

101

think you can tie it around you?" he called again. I nodded again, though I was sure I'd never be able to lift a finger.

The kids' voices faded and down came the rope. Well, the end was tied in a loop, thank God, so I just sort of slithered in one arm, then the other, my heart pounding and leaning all my weight into the wall. I don't really know how I managed to get into it. They tugged on the rope, the other guy called ready, I nodded, and up, very slowly, I came.

Alright, alright, my friend Buddy – no such luck for him, yes, he died, instantly I hope.

Why on earth did we do it, I shook my head.

"You just told the story... I know why you did it....didn't you listen to anything you said?" she asked.

# Time Line

Now me, I'm a punctual person. I pride myself on being on time. But my old friend Joan, look, I shake my head just thinking how she's always late. Her mother says she was born late and she's been late ever since. Don't get me wrong. I still think the world of her, but that woman can't leave her house just once – she always has to go back in for something! My God, I'm starting to chew a nail, just thinking about how Joanie treats time. Still, we have a lot in common – I mean, I enjoy her company.

She was the first kid in our class to receive a watch. It didn't take her long to fix that. You know what she would do if she knew she was going to be late, say, coming home from skating…she'd just turn the hands back…can you imagine that?

But that time in Montreal though, I'm sure it wouldn't have helped. We weren't playing with time. Time played with us. Or was it the goddess' guiding hand? I don't know! Want to hear about it? First, let me see if I have time.

We were both seventeen, visiting from a small town in N.B. Now, if we'd been ten, I could see why we'd think this was a magical happening – the story I'm about to tell you. But we were almost grown up, if there is any such thing, which there isn't. I don't think I'm cynical, just realistic. Anyway, we were naïve and just inexperienced in big city life.

We stayed with relatives of Joanie's in Point Claire, a suburb of Montreal you know. Every day, we'd take this little commuter train into the CP station, below the Queen Elizabeth Hotel. They put this on especially for summer visitors. From there it was a ten minute walk, may be a little less, to catch the Metro, which took us directly to the Isle St. Helene and La Ronde, the fun part supposedly. I say supposedly because…well, you'll see. We were with Joanie's parents, though this particular night, they'd let us out on our own. After all, were 17 – Joanie could even drive a car.

We had secretly planned to go to La Ronde, where we'd read about all the nightclubs – though now, I'm not even sure they existed!

Oh, what time is it getting to be? Oh, I'd better speed things up because I have a rendezvous and, you guessed it, I want to be on time.

So where was I – oh, when I think of it, that girl could be so exasperating – look, now I'm twisting my chain. Anyway, that night, I had to wait for her, as usual. Finally, we left. It was just down the street, the little commuter train, and we almost missed it. Not that we were in a hurry, but you know, the best place to wait for the train is at the station. But I'll try to shorten up this story. We arrived at La Ronde about 8…:17, it was.

I remember Joanie complaining, it was too early to go clubbing, which was true, but that girl just despised being early – or even on time.

"What's on time?" she'd say.

When people expect you, I'd say. The time they say, I'd explain.

"But people don't really want you there at 8:30, say, at a party, they just want you there any time after," she'd say.

Now, can you understand that way of thinking? Do trains or buses invite you for after, I'd say.

"That's different and you know it," she'd say. "I wouldn't be late for a plane or a train."

Hah, my foot she wouldn't. Two years in a row at Christmas time, Joanie arrived home an entire day late from university. Why? Because she hitchhiked to catch the train further up the tracks! Does that make sense to you? Oh, look at my chain – all twisted up – just talking about travel connections makes me nervous. But I'm getting way off track, so to speak! I guess I have a few bad habits myself. Where was I? Oh, we were at La Ronde – Joanie complaining, there's no one here. True, the place was deserted. "And we have to leave early to get back to Pt. Claire." Really, at 17, you'd think we were regular clubbers, the way we carried on.

Anyway, we wandered around, looking at the empty rides. It had rained at suppertime. There were lots of puddles around and it was a lovely mild night for late September. We stood on tiptoes and peered into windows and strained our ears trying to hear music – a club would have music, right? I'm still not sure if there were boîtes de nuit down there. Oh, what time is it – I'm taking so long I won't have time to tell the real story.  OK, I'll squeeze it all into the next four minutes, because then, I have to go!

OK, we hadn't found a club. We contemplated our next move, sitting on huge rocks down by the water. I asked my favourite question – what time is it? Then I went, "what time does that last commuter train leave?"

Eleven eleven, she said, smart as anything. It's 10:50 now – think we should go? It all comes back so clearly – as if everything was in suspended animation, so to speak. Do you believe time can stand still? I made a rapid calculation in my head – Joanie must have been doing the same thing because we were off those rocks in a flash and running to where we had to get the Metro.

Of course, it wasn't there waiting for us. My heart was pounding. I was tapping my foot, chewing my nails and asking what time it was every few seconds. Now Joanie is very good under pressure – just as calm as anything – till it's all over. She was standing there blathering away.

"What would we do if we got stuck in downtown Montreal overnight," she says.

Probably get murdered, I remember answering.

"Don't be silly," she says. Her eyes were twinkling. She was looking forward to it. "I have an idea," she says, we could go to a 24 hour restaurant."

I could have throttled her then. I didn't want to sit in some godforsaken restaurant all night, all alone – or worse yet, with some old drunks hanging around us. I had an idea. What about your parents, I asked, thinking, you know, that might jolt her into reality…trying to make her as scared as I was I guess.

"Oh," she says, "we'll have to phone and explain we missed the train. They'll be fine as long as they know where we are."

Well, back then, that answer made perfect sense to me. But now, as a mother, if I knew my daughter was wandering around in a strange city with no place to go, I'd go out of my mind. Then again, it didn't dawn on either of us that one of Joanie's relatives could just drive in and pick us up – imagine!

The next thing Joanie said was, "hey, maybe we could go clubbing in downtown Montreal."

Good thing for her the Metro pulled up. We hopped on – not another soul on the train, it being the end of the line after all. Then, that damn train just sat there, waiting - time was ticking away…I sat there squirming in my seat when finally the doors hissed shut and the car backed up – you know how the subway does that, like a runner crouches, rises, then takes off.

Then Joan, look, I'm chewing a nail again, Joan says, "look at all the lights of the city" you know, just completely oblivious to our predicament. There I was, dreading not making it home, and there she was, relishing the thought of wandering the streets of Montreal all night.

So, I have to finish the story now. Alright, it was 11:09 as we lit out from the metro. Funny, we both knew it was impossible to catch that train but we started racing down the street anyway. Funny too because, for all our differences, we were suddenly completely of one mind. Now me, I'm long-legged but my friend Joanie's just a short little thing. But when we got going, we just ran like the wind – it felt like we were being propelled along by some unseen force. We had about three blocks to go, then there was the park. It had a hedge all around it, but somehow, we breezed through an opening, then we just hurdled over every bush and flowerbed in our path – just like gazelles, in one easy motion. Then we shot through a break in the hedge and found ourselves on the sidewalk – no traffic – we kept right on moving into the gaping hole that used to be the entrance to the station. Then...look, I shake my head as I see it all over again – we had to go up an escalator. It was like a chase in a movie scene – up, hands gripping the rail, dashing around the odd person. Nowadays, you know, everyone stands politely to the right to let the people in a hurry, the frantics, Joanie calls them, but back then, everyone just enjoyed the ride!

At the top, we looked around, then dashed across a big open area and burst through a door. We were outside – it was night, with a bulb burning here and there. There were train tracks and a sooty smell mixed in with the fresh air. Over on the last set of tracks was our train – steam was puffing out of it, sort of outlining it you know, and it was rolling away, already a few yards down the track. A trainman, yes, a trainman was standing on those steps at the end of it...waving at us, just as if he'd been expecting us. We were both speeding toward it...ever jumped on a moving train? Well, first you have to be running at the same speed as it, then you give a little burst, grab the bar and pull – up. The trainman stretched out a hand to help Joanie. Once she was on, he reached down and helped me on. The train was already picking up speed but we'd made it!

I was trying to catch my breath. I looked over at Joanie – she was doubled over and shaking. I thought she was crying - should have known better. The little brat was laughing – she looked at me, it's catching you know. I'm sure mine was hysterical laughter. The trainman even joined in. I'm sure he knew the whole situation.

But, how did we make it – was the train late? What drove us to keep going? Did time stand still? I don't know to this day.

Oh my goodness – what time is it? Ahh, I have to pick up my daughter. Oh well, I don't know why I bother hurrying – that girl is always late!

# Red Rose Tea

**A**unt Irene is always playing cards, mostly bridge, but she plays other games too. She taught me how to play Gin Rummy and Solitaire, which is probably her second most favourite game. People go to visit her and they play cards. I have tea with her sometimes after school. Maybe I'll go today, if there are no cars in her driveway. She saves the bird cards from the Red Rose tea boxes for me. She laughs a lot and never gets upset at all and ... she's fun.

I think I will go see her now. Hey, I don't have to stand on tiptoes to reach the horseshoe-shaped door knocker. She's the only person I know who has a knocker. Tap, tap and one harder tap, in case – Aunt Irene is hard of hearing.

The door scrapes over the carpet and there she is, peeking out and smiling. "Why it's Connie. Hi honey, coming to visit?"

"Hi Aunt Irene. Sure, if you don't have company."

"Why no, I haven't. Come on in. Have time for a cup of tea?"

"Sure, I'd love some." Aunt Irene lets me drink real tea with her. "But I'd better call home and see if it's alright with Mummy."

"O.K. dear, I'll put the kettle on while you do that."

Aunt Irene has a pink phone, a Touch Tone, she calls it, to go with her rugs. We have a black dial phone on the wall.

"Mummy says I have to be home by four-thirty. I can tell time now Aunt Irene. See – it's ten after three."

"Good, we'll have time for tea and a nice long chat." Aunt Irene goes back to the chair at her round red table, which I love. She's playing a game of bridge. I can tell that because there are four hands on the table. "Pick up that hand Connie, and you can help me finish the game."

I climb up on the red cushioned bench built curved into the corner. "I can hardly hold all these cards in my hands, Aunt Irene, there are so many."

"That's because your hands are so little, honey. Here, try holding them a little closer together." She folds the cards, then spreads them out with a flick of her fingers, at the top only.

"Yes, that's a lot better."

"OK. Now, do you have the Ace of Spades?"

I sit up with a start.

"Yes, how did you know that, Aunt Irene?"

"Oh, card sense dear. You pull that out and play it."

"Now," she says, "play your King."

I have that too! "Aunt Irene, did you already look at my cards?"

She throws her head back in her high-pitched squeaky laugh. "No, dear, just years of practice." Then she slides around the red table and picks up the other hand beside me. She looks at it quickly, draws out two cards, puts the cards down, then settles back in her own chair. She looks quickly at her cards, folds them, then reaches over for the fourth hand. "OK, now play your lowest black card – do you have the three or four of clubs or spades?"

I'm astonished again. "Yes, I have the four of clubs."

"Throw it out."

Aunt Irene hums while she's thinking about her next move. She names everything she wants played and we finish the game. "Would you pull the plug on the kettle, Connie, but be careful!"

"Sure." I climb down and walk over to the red counter. This house is so quiet too, compared to our house. We have five kids talking at the top of their lungs, squealing, fighting and running around in the house all day, my mother says. While I'm up on the chair to unplug the kettle, I spy two empty lawn chairs down by the garage.

"Hey, Aunt Irene, why don't we have tea outside today? See the two chairs?"

"What a lovely idea honey. And I have an even better place for tea. Let me see, we need a tray. Connie, would you go to the living room and bring me a TV table. Just pull it off, you'll see, and we'll put everything we need on it. Off you go."

My feet feel like they're sinking and floating at the same time, on the carpet through the hall. There's the curving stairway, pink rugs on it too. I think I'll go up. It feels like rising to heaven, my body feels so light, turn, then down again, floating gently. Does everything curve in this house? Even Aunt Irene's picture window is rounded outwards – a bow window, it's called. Our picture windows are flat. Oh, I forgot to ask Aunt Irene if she has any new bird cards. Here are the tables, hanging. They look like little birds' feet wrapped around a branch. Sure enough, one top pulls off easily.

I can hear Aunt Irene humming as I pad through the hall. Ah, there's my favourite of Aunt Irene's teapots. She has three or four. This one looks like a target for arrows. It has red and white circles going up it. I place the tray on the counter. She's already poured a little hot water into the pot to warm it up. Now she moves the pot around in a circle a few times, dumps it into the sink, pops a tea bag in, and fills the pot with boiling water. "Connie, let me see, I think I might have a mocha cake or two left."

"Oh goodie, yes please Aunt Irene. We never have them at our house."

"Now, are we ready – I have the tea and sweets on the tray. Oh, I have some bird cards for you Connie. Good, pull hard on the sun porch door."

"Over to the right, Connie, not down there."

"What's this Aunt Irene, I didn't know you had this nice little patch of lawn, surrounded by all those bushes. Are those roses? Gee, this is just like another room, Aunt Irene, three walls of roses and the sun porch is the fourth wall."

Aunt Irene has two big white wooden chairs, deep, with high rounded backs, and a table to match.

"There, you sit in that chair, this one will be mine. Hmm, why don't you sit on the arm of the chair, Connie, you might get lost way down there."

I scramble up onto the arm. "This chair's big enough for three kids. Now I can see better too. Umm, it smells so good in here."

"Here honey, have a look at the bird cards while I pour the tea. If you already have them, I'll give them to Gregory. "

"Oh, I didn't know he collected bird cards too. A robin, I already have that one, and a blue jay, I have that. A hummingbird, hummm, do you suppose it really hums? Look at this strange looking little bird, Aunt Irene – look, its beak looks like a darning needle." I hold the card to show her, then bring it back to examine it again." Its wings are see-through. And look at the red throat. Did you ever see a hummingbird Aunt Irene?"

"Let me have a good look, Connie. No, I don't think I ever have."

"Do you think one would ever come around here?"

"Well, I've noticed a lot of birds on those cards don't live around here. Why don't you read the back of the card, doesn't it usually say where in North America they're found?"

"OK, here, you look at the map and I'll read the card. After all, I'll be finished grade two tomorrow. Can you tell where it's found?"

"Yes, southern Canada and all over the U.S. OK, here, you read."

"It says, ruby-throated hummingbird. Needle-like bill. Between 2 and 3 and a half inches. Tiny. Gee, how big is that Aunt Irene?"

Aunt Irene holds up her thumb and first finger, indicating the size. And what else does it say, Connie?"

Metal – lic green above, white below. Above what – oh, its head and back. Male has brill-i-ant red throat. Right, ruby-throated. Makes a humming sound with its wings, which accounts for its name. It is often found around red tub-u-lar flowers. What's tub-u-lar mean?"

"Hmm, let me see the card honey. Oh, tube – tubular. Sort of deep, tube-like." She returns the card.

"Makes a little squeaking sound, like a mouse. Of course, it's as small as a mouse. Would roses be tubular, Aunt Irene?"

"Oh, not really dear. Well, maybe now, in the early stages. Ready for some tea with milk?"

"Yes please."

"Ah, perfect, Aunt Irene. Not too hot."

"Cake?"

"Yes please. I wish my mother knew how to make these."

A sudden whir makes my back straighten. I've already had a run-in with a bumblebee this year. A sharp, darting movement draws my eye. It looks like a big fat bee, then I see the needle-like beak. I flap my hand, because my mouth is full, trying to get Aunt Irene's attention, and not wanting to make a sound.

We both watch the tiny bird. It darts to one rose, inserts its bill, wings vibrating, withdraws and flits to a new flower, then glides backwards to another, nosing it and humming all the while. Then it needles to a fourth mass of red. With one squeak, it dips, bounds upward and disappears.

I can't believe my eyes. My heart lifts and I feel like I'm going to float way. My mouth turns into a big smile. My head turns to see Aunt Irene. She has a faraway look in her eyes, then she dips her head, looking at me over the top of her glasses, smiling too, and shaking her head. We sip our tea, munch our mocha cakes. Only at Aunt Irene's would this ever happen, I think.

## Margo's Mother

Dark muscled thunderclouds towered in the eastern sky, immovable in the hot humid breezeless air. Martha was visiting her sister Nancy. Bobby had finished mowing the cottage lawn. Nancy had invited him onto the roof-covered porch for tea. Cinnamon and peach tea alright?

Don't you have regular tea? Bobby shook his head.

Yes, but we're having something new today – suit you?

OK. Guess I'll take what's on offer.

Nancy stepped into the cottage to prepare tea. She came back to the porch with teapot and three cups in hand, set them down and poured. A low grumble rolled their way.

Sounds like we might get a show, Nance nodded toward the sky. Her guests agreed. Bobby swept his hands up and down his bare arms.

What's that thing you're wearing Bob, around your neck?

He put his thumb beneath the necklace and pulled it out. It's magnetic. For arthritis. I wear it when I'm getting a bit stiff – usually tells me when it's going to rain. Could today – look at them clouds – he flicked a hand up beyond his right shoulder.

Yes, there's potential and we need rain God knows. Magnetic eh? What's it supposed to do – balance your ions?

Something like that, Bobby held out his empty teacup.

Nance nodded, I find it tasty. Mart, what about you?

Yes, it's good. So what's on your mind today Nance?

Well, I'd love to tell this story about my friend Margo and her mother, who died last winter. She poured more tea and handed Bob and Martha their cups.

Does either of you believe in reincarnation – that's sort of what it involves I think.

What...? Bobby sputtered into his tea. Incarn ... reincarnation … come off it, that's a pile of horseshit.

You know my answer Sis, Catholics don't believe in it. And anyway, what does reincarnation mean?

It means the living spirit of one whose physical body dies enters another being, Nance said. To be born into another body. The thunder groaned again in the distance.

You're not going to believe this but I swear it's all true.

Wait, entering another being? Human or what? Mart wanted to know.

I don't really know – in this case, animal, Nance's voice went up slightly to a question.

And what happens to the spirit of the new being – just shoved aside while the old spirit takes over? Oh Nancy, you really do get some fanciful ideas, Mart added.

Well, sense is not part of the equation, Nancy said thoughtfully. It is unexplainable – there's no logic to it. A flash of lightning streaked the sky, followed by a rumble.

I understand there are paradoxes in life, no question about that, but … I just find reincarnation impossible to fathom, Martha said with a little irritation in her voice. As far as I'm concerned, it cannot exist. Amen. The thunder gargled louder now.

What about you Bob?

No, once you're dead, that's it, the end! I believe in dancing and having a good time in this life but once you're dead, you're dead. There ain't nothin' after that, they put you in the ground...or burn you up – that's it. He leaned back with his tea cup, looking quite satisfied. Martha sat, lips pressed together. The clouds groaned ever nearer.

You don't believe in an afterlife Bobby? I thought everybody did by now. There are so many stories...you know, the tunnel of white light … dead family members with outstretched arms, to welcome the newly departed. So I guess you don't really want to hear this story I was going to tell.

Ah well, alright. I'll listen to a story – just don't expect me to believe it. Marty adjusted her skirt.

Nance refilled their teacups. A loud crack and a flash followed by louder rumbling came from the east. The air felt suddenly cooler.

I hope this keeps up so we finally get rid of this dratted humidity, Nance announced.

Here here, Mart and Bobby nodded. Come on Nance, tell the story.

OK ready for this? My friend Margo's mother was dying. She was pure love, according to Margo. She and her mother are very much alike, but express things differently.

Bobby looked at her. Now what in hell does that mean?

I mean, though they are both very determined people, Mrs. Simmons was neat as a pin, while Margo is at the other end of the spectrum - driven to keep things messy. But that is neither here nor there. They did have, still have, a strong bond, as you will see.

First, a little background. Margo's mother loved animals, birds, people and plants. And they loved her. She always had cats and birdfeeders out around her house. Her home was surrounded by beautiful bushes and a great expanse of lawn – where lived lots of worms to feed the robins, her favourite bird.

But Mrs. Simmons' life was ebbing from her. She was in bed, too weak to walk. She was eighty-five – and still always in good humour. She and I had had a very good chat about a month before, about her daughter. My friend Margo is kind of a wanderer – she can help others, gives great advice, but has a hard time dealing with herself. Anyway, I'd told Mrs. Simmons that her other friends and I would look after her. Mrs. Simmons looked me in the eye, comprehending me perfectly.

But I'll get on with the story. So, Margo was understandably distressed when her mother was about to take her leave. In their final exchanges, she told her mother she would miss her terribly. Mrs Simmons, a woman of faith, assured her she would be around, watching over her. How would she know, Margo wanted to know. You'll know, her mother told her. Hey, you two still with me?

Bobby nodded, looking out at the trees with a faraway look in his eyes. Martha sipped her tea, listening carefully.

Well, about a month after Mrs. Simmons died, so mid-February, Margo drove up to Bouctouche from Moncton, to check on her mother's house, which was closed up for winter. It was Margo's now. The day was freezing cold, like minus 25, as cold and dry and bright as it is hot and humid and dark here today. Margo was bereft, very sad, had hardly left her apartment for a month, but ... something drew her out. A thunderous clap and flash together lit up the dark sky. A few raindrops splattered on the roof.

Yow, we might really get rain but back to the story! The sun was glinting off the snow which covered all but the tops of the rose bushes. The bare branches of Mrs. Simmons' silverbush protruded above the snow. The birch tree stood alone next to the garage. Fortunately, the wind had blown part of the driveway clear. Margo got out of her car, the quiet surrounding her.

She was fitting the key into the lock when she heard a scraping sound like someone making a snowball. She turned to see a bird burst up out of the snow and light on the bottom branch of the birch. Then it sang, loud and clear. Not a chickadee, she told me, the bird we hear around New Brunswick in winter. The bird tweeted a long song again. Margo recognized the tune, a robin, singing to her.

Ha, there's where you must be wrong, Bobby was smiling. Robins don't winter in New Brunswick.

And you're right Bob, they don't. But there it was, a robin, Mrs. Simmons' favourite bird. It was Mrs. Simmons herself, according to Margo. Margo says she was saying to her, "perk up, perk up, I'm just fine, perk up and get on with your life!

You don't expect me to believe her mother became a robin do you? Bobby looked to Martha for support.

Martha's mouth was slightly agape – but then she said, My Lord, I just remembered a very similar thing happened to my friend Linda who was widowed last fall. She'd just asked for a sign that she was going to be O.K. and poof, she looked up and there was a robin – sitting on the railing of her back deck, in the middle of winter.

Wow – now that's fascinating too! Two quick flashes of lightning lit up the sky. Cracks of thunder were so loud, the three felt their chairs vibrate. More big drops hit the roof.

Hey, I think we may witness a great storm here. Bobby rubbed his bare arms again.

Well, tell me what you make of this last part now that we've also heard Mart's story – still interested?

O.K. go – then I have to go! Enough of this ghosty stuff! Then added, my mother used to say that when she died, she hoped my father would be there waiting for her. But I don't believe in such foolishness.

Oh never mind Bob – only a believer could appreciate this story. Marty – you interested?

I'm listening Nance, Martha said. Her forehead crinkled to a question mark. I wonder...

You wonder what Marty? Nance stopped.

Ah, I don't know yet – go on Nance.

O.K. Last week, I hadn't talked to Margo for several days. Normally, we talk at least every couple. I was sitting on the front porch when this robin came into view, bobbing and walking along the driveway in front of me, chirping and tweeting quite insistently. I knew it was Mrs. Simmons telling me to contact Margo! I did phone and sure enough, Margo was feeling rather depressed. Now tell me there's not something in that!

Gee – I don't know Nancy. Everything comes in threes they say. Bob crooked his head to one side.

Martha suddenly sat up, smiling. Did you mention providence? That sounds like providence to me but ...maybe the robin is actually Mrs. Simmons' emissary – have you thought of that Nance?

Lightning lit up the whole sky, the thunder cracked so loudly, the three came to their feet. Bobby's hair was standing straight up. He reached for his necklace. Holy, feel that – it's warm, almost hot. Think they're trying to tell us something, cracked Bob, wide-eyed.

Just you Bob, Martha said.

*Untitled # 2, Roméo Savoie, 2012*

# Roméo Savoie

## Interview

**1)** I would like to ask you a few questions concerning your practice as an artist. What is this act called creativity for an artist? For instance, Julian Schnabel says something like, "I want to do a painting that I can look at."

This simple answer says everything. An artist is trained to do art and this process exhibits his tastes, good or bad. Apart from his training comes talent and work. Talent is beyond teaching and comes mostly from his tradition. Once he or she is trained we can see the result through the work process. The talent is, in other words, revealed. The work process eliminates what is considered useless.

2) Do we know where this act comes from?

I've used the word "tradition" a while ago. I think that a person is born with certain capacities, and through living, talents are revealed. Then comes what is natural. Can this talent be developed in this life setting? If so, one must get the proper schooling.

3) Why were you compelled to leave architecture to become an artist in painting?

What was revealed to me in Europe when I went there in 1964 is that I preferred art works to buildings. I could appreciate a wonderful building by Le Corbusier, Nervi, Gaudi, etc., but was drawn to what I didn't know: Soulages, the Cobra Group, etc. I remember seeing a small painting in Amsterdam and decided then and there that the challenge of painting was greater than the one presented to be by architecture. I was trained to understand the creative process in building design and not in painting. I saw with my eyes what my mind didn't understand.

4) What subjects do you address in your painting?

119

Traditional painters had subjects that they treated: portraits, landscapes, still life, etc., but I was interested in what I saw in the School of New York. With Rauschenberg, Jasper Johns, Black Mountain College, Marcel Duchamp, etc., appeared a baroque attitude to the surface that was treated, baroque meaning everything. All materials available were used on the surface and around that surface. Real objects were added instead of being painted. This liberty in conception initiated installations. So I work in the same way. Being in the studio in front of a canvas will trigger actions that are transferred onto that surface and the process continues until I'm satisfied with what is there. I've used objects such as pianos, fans, flowers, blackboards, ladders, hopscotch, trees, etc., or just colour with sand or gravel or encaustic. The ideas change as one paints.

5) Some say that you prefer painting with black. Is that a fact?

Black is intriguing because of its reference to writing. Japanese Zen masters used India ink to transfer calligraphic symbols and I do admire the elegance of these markings. I check everything around me, all the symbols, the markings on walls, the lines on a building, etc. All these markings are registered in the mind and reappear on a painting. It seems to be a logical process. But every mind is different, each hand writing, symbols used or desires or preferences also. What is transferred is a temporary choice relating to some image or emotion. It is immediate and sometimes it has no direct meaning.

6) Why do you do series instead of individual paintings?

Working in series is what happens. Let us say that I start by spreading colour, because I don't have a subject. While painting, the name of a city like Venice appears in my mind. So I write the name on the colour. From that moment I am aware or become aware of a subject; the name of a city. If I think of Venice (I have been there a few times), I can imagine the structure of that city that is on the sea. I can imagine a cross section of that concept, above and below the horizon. So the painting is translated in two parts, the lower part darker than the upper part. I was also fascinated by the idea that buildings had openings above the canals, as tides vary and gondolas or boats are like our cars. These ideas are translated in symbols. Now, that one painting is solved. I wonder if I could translate the name of another city in a painting? Let us say that I think of Toronto because I have a close friend there. This is the beginning of a series because I want to try it with other names like Paris, London, New York and Kouchibouguac, etc.

7) You did write a poem called Kouchibouguac. Is there a link between the poem and the painting?

I was in Montreal when I wrote that poem. I was called to participate in a poetic reading at the same time as I was doing a painting in my studio. So while painting, I would take breaks and write about the energy around me and the paintings and that invitation. When it was finished I called it Kouchibouguac because of the words and the images used. First, I didn't agree with the fact that a government could eliminate two or three villages where people lived, to make a park. At the reading I accompanied the words with slides and music, music by Avro Pärt and slides that I had taken of overturned boats. It was more like a performance piece.

8) In writing, is the subject always imposed before starting?

Not really. I write with a typewriter, in front of a screen or sitting in a café. The energy around me varies. In front of a typewriter I can hear the clicking of the "touch". I am in a private setting as when I am in front of a computer. Each sound or image triggers words in the brain (3 or 4 per second) and one is chosen during that process. If I am in a café, motions of people and sounds of speaking or music trigger other words. The mind becomes a computer and words carry the energies around me. As an instrument I record with words what is going on in my head. Of course, I've been reading poetry since the age of 15, mainly all the French poets. I am fascinated by the poetic mind, so as a creative person, what happens, happens I suppose. For instance, if I like a writer like Marguerite Duras, I will read all of her books. If I like a composer like Ravel, I will listen for a time to all his music. They help me tolerate what I see and hear that is intolerable.

9) Could you live without them, I mean these writers and composers?

I cannot imagine what it would be like without them. You see, I'm trained as a visual artist and as an architect. That creates a sort of ideology of existence. My world is shared with artists, writers and thinkers. That is the world that I live in. I read, paint and write.

10) You seem to be a solitary person.

I suppose so, as compared with people who go to work all day with other people. I go to work with myself – I could be considered a solitary person.

11) When you work in your studio do you listen to music for instance on the radio?

The radio could be a distraction for sure. The work is in two parts: the creative time and the execution time. If I'm creating a piece, I can't be distracted by sounds. But after, if I'm only putting a colour on a canvas or a primer, it doesn't matter. Sometimes we do need a force to accompany us, some force that will push us into action, like listening to Martha Argerich. Her playing is so outstanding that it may help us reach towards excellence. It's that kind of an idea.

12) It must be extremely difficult to isolate oneself to do work.

People are isolated all the time. I chose to work as a creative artist because it fulfills me. Isolation is part of the process. I really don't mind it, in fact I think that it's necessary. I've seen carpenters erecting a building and even though it's noisy, they don't see or hear you when you approach. I probably don't need things moving around or sounds bouncing off walls when I'm in that process. Isolation is fine.

13) How do you discipline yourself to do this kind of work?

Maybe you need a form of distraction to do your work. Your body/mind is different than mine. It's training. I'm trained to do the type of work that I do. If you're a pianist for instance (I lived with one, once), these people can sit at the piano for 4 hours banging on keys. Secretaries bang on typewriters, carpenters on nails. Maybe my ears are sensitive so my banging is done with brushes.

14) How do others see you?

Others? I have no idea. They come to shows and look and look, trying to understand what is going on. It reminds me when I was in Paris in 1964 looking at paintings by Soulages that consisted of wide brushstrokes of black paint on large white canvases. Not one painting, but a whole show at the Grand Palais. That was a revelation it had to be serious because Grand Palais is a prominent exhibition hall. Yes, I had to stop and work it out. My responsibility is doing paintings. What others think is not important.

15) So how do you handle a professional critique?

Well, I don't have to worry about that here. Journalists report what they see. If I have a show in a larger city, Montreal for instance, where I spent nineteen years and my shows were reported in art magazines, generally the comments are interesting and professional. I've never really had a negative report on my shows or my work. Most of them came to my master's degree exhibition and knew of my work.

16) What about galleries? Do they critique your work or show you work?

Galleries are made to see art. If a gallery represents you, usually they like your work. But if they can't see, then the rapport is tepid. They love to sell, so the more they sell, the more they love you. I do art for my reasons and they sell art for their reasons.

17) Let us go back to writing. I've noticed that your first book, "Duo de Demesure," is written in a different way than the others. Can you explain that?

"Duo de Demesure" is a performance piece and my other books of poetry are about poetry, so the writing is different. In a novel or in critical writing, the structure varies automatically, the choice of words also. It's adjusting the words to the concept.

18) Is the concept of writing the same as in painting?

Intellectually, it could be coming from the same source, one source using words and the other, colours. If you're thinking about results,

123

then it depends on the training and the ability, which means the talent of the artist. These vary quite a bit. Some paint to sell, so the direction depends on the client. Others paint to learn and that is altogether another concept.

19) So, you do insist on training.

It seems obvious to me. Our society operates that way. Doctors, lawyers, nurses, truck drivers, barbers, etc., all of them are trained. If you're driving an expensive car, are you going to let an inexperienced person fool around with the motor or go to a plumber for a tooth extraction? Of course there are amateurs out there, in every field in fact, but they will not change or be part of the history of art. Some may be cited in a section called naïve art. But that also is a very specific way of painting.

20) What about textures in your paintings, are they necessary?

You are probably referring to traditional oil on canvas paintings that are smooth. Textures were introduced mainly by the School of New York in the fifties. Anselm Keifer, one of my references in art, uses textures that can be two or three inches thick. Now, does that change the artistic value of the painting? It doesn't affect national museums, for instance. Yes, I use textures when it is needed.

21) But some of the particles may fall off the painting. Does that worry you?

I don't see why I should be worried. It is also part of the process. Of course, some of the particles may fall off. If some are offended by it, so be it. I can't change the world.

22) But if someone doesn't buy your painting because of a fragile surface, doesn't that offend you?

Look, art is not about selling or conservation. I am not there when I work and I can't change or want to change where some of the people are, in their evaluation of excellence. That is not my function.

23) Doesn't an artist have to explain his work?

Have to explain his work? No. But I often spend time when asked, to show slides of my work. If that question arises in the conversation, of course I will address it. I will not defend it one way or another. I will explain what I do and why I do it and let "people" be what they are. As I said before, I don't want to change the world.

24) Tell me, who are the artists that influence you.

Everything we see around us influences us but some artists are closer to us than others. I call it references. So these references are multiple of course, but I must say that Robert Rauschenberg was the first artist that stunned me, that stopped me when walking through a museum for instance. Quickly, others: Antoni Tàpies from Spain, Anselm Keifer from Germany and Julian Schnabel from New York. I really love their work.

25) Why is that?

There is a link between their vision and mine. Why do we have preferences in music, literature, in all the arts in general? These preferences indicate where you are in life.

26) Some say that putting oneself under the influence of another is copying.

Nobody can make a Rauschenberg other than Rauschenberg. So, using someone's influence is being stimulated by someone else's work. We know nothing, so we use others to advance in life. It's like eliminating certain aspects of the whole picture so that you can proceed in other areas.

27) In an art process what place do you give to negative forces that can invade the work?

It's an eliminating process. I may want to add an object, a colour or a texture while painting and discover that it doesn't work, so it is covered over or scratched out – eliminated. It isn't a problem, it's how it works. You work that surface until you're satisfied.

28) What subjects do you use in your paintings?

Anything can be used that makes sense. India ink refers to writing. Colour represents itself in that red is a warm colour, blue and green are cold. An event may suggest a title and this title can be written on the painting. Nature can be used as symbols, trees representing life, etc. When a symbol appears in the painting process, it must be treated to understand why it is there, what position it occupies so that the environment can adjust itself to this object or symbol.

29) In some of your paintings like in the series called, "Mémoire de Ville", we see lacerations in the wood surface. Can you explain?

On a canvas, one doesn't cut into the surface like Fontana. Generally a brush mark would be used. But on wood, these markings can be cut into the wood. So it is done because of the possibility that surface offers. When we think of drawing we think of paper. But as children, if we wanted to draw a heart with an initial in it, we often found harder surfaces like trees to show that the message is a permanent one. We only repeat what we have learned and sometimes reinforce the gesture to make a point.

30) So do you use accidents when painting like spilling or dropping a brush filled with ink, etc.?

I use these accidents as subconscious creative moments. It sounds snobbish to say it this way but in my process every gesture is considered be it conscious or subconscious. Every gesture comes from the same body. As I said before, when something doesn't work it is eliminated. A dropped brush might make a mark that is acceptable.

31) In 1964, you traveled through Europe for a year and in 1970, you stayed in a studio for 18 months in Aix en Provence. How did this change your painting?

In '64 it was more about visiting Europe, but in 1970 I spent 18 months working only on gestural paintings, like making scales on a piano for four hours. I had to learn to write with paint. There's another aspect that needs to be mentioned. Being in a richer cultural environment broadens your vision on reality. For that reason alone, being in a strange space helped me concentrate on the artistic values as a whole. In Europe, history is everywhere. You have to adjust. From my studio I could see "La Sainte Victoire" that Cézanne painted and I had a studio "au Chateau Noir" that he also painted. Your attitude is quite different in that type of setting. I could go to a library and find a signed book of an important poet. That changes everything. Here your history is short and your references, limited. In France you walk in a small village and find a Roman church from the XIIth century. That is amazing.

## Out of Whiteness

Out of this whiteness
Out of touch out of fear
Like little fireflies trembling
Like fingers running away
On grand pianos
Making melodies and sounds
Running away

Out of this darkness
Into fluid skies
Nothing is valid
Only burned torches
And songs left behind
While marching and marching
In shadows of nothingness

Out in the open
Under clouds and branches
Lifting from the ground
Fallen leaves and willows
Under all the nonsense
And broken dreams
What is left but emptiness

Mapped strategies in foul
Odours from overturned lichen
I remember walking slowly
More slowly than pigeons
Or other birds that come
And go like forgotten songs
That disappear in stillness

The caravan moves on
Heading towards the desert
Where nothing grows
But melancholy or dry thoughts
Filled with shadows

And passing orangs-outans
Circling unturned stones

Someone will come
In abstract nights
Turning slivers of sweetness
Into shards of thoughts
Unfinished concepts disappear
Into stillness
Silence becomes one's religion

Closeness stands still
Brushing away thoughts of war
And other securities
Into the white mist
Lights that appear
And fade into darkness

## Lemond, or Life Will Get You

One looks up at the sky
Wishing for swallows and giant birds
Wishing for other places like China
Love is like a pinnacle on top of large buildings
Shimmering in gold light one cannot reach

Strangers pass and wander into the mist
Looking like lost politicians
Thinking that this could be the spot to smile
At some worthy cause like saving
Santa from small chimneys at Christmas

Wanting wanting wanting
A Cadillac car   a yellow bird
Wanting a voice like Sinatra
Or a suit from Armani
Life is such a dull place
When bars close at two and
Girls go home sober

The sky is peppered with balloon clouds
Pines sway to and fro saying nothing
While across the way poets rearrange
Shelves from IKEA with instructions
As thick as Webster's Dictionary

The world does go round and round
Finally it may pick you up
And sway you to and fro
Like a lifeless scarecrow in a corn field
Scaring all the children that call
For their mummies when afraid
Scarecrows are just old clothes on a stick
But it works on children and not so much
On birds   life is funny that way

Lessons can be learned from little events

Not always in school where it should be
But by eating jello or slipping on a brown spot
Or walking on cracks or straying in the traffic
Or saying the wrong word at breakfast
Or not flushing or eating chocolates
With a wedding gown or borrowing your
Mother's pearls or smoking under the covers

Life will get you one way or another

Some stories are shorter than others
And some sad and tearful
But life is a howl listening to children
Seeing fat people trip on twine
Or thin people walk like sticks
Or dogs chasing seagulls near the sea
Or hummingbirds chasing hummingbirds
Or racoons climbing posts for birdseeds

Cats are the funniest   they'll jump
On forbidden objects the moment
You turn around   run away from strangers
And jump on their lap while they sit to eat
Bring you a mouse after breakfast
And meow their way in or out
Indifferent, nonchalant as kings
Or stars they contemplate like gurus
And never come when you call

It rains still   finding cracks near chimneys
And drip while you sleep or while
Running for pots   while seeing your favourite
Blouse on the clothesline or an open window
In your car at the road or near your
Favourite painting while the TV announcer
Tells you to keep smiling while you trip
On the wet mop in the hall

Life will get you one way or another

*Black and White Series # 4, Nancy King Schofield, 2012*

# Nancy King Schofield

## Interrupted Flight

I carry your tiny body
bone china light
as air in feather cups
on outstretched arms

victim of a cosmic spectral
you were dazzled by its beauty
scintillating and hypnotic
that held you spellbound

in a shimmering
that made you spin
corkscrew carving through
walls of cobalt blue

an astral knife
that sliced and shredded
discarded sky litter
until colliding

with the unexpected
stopped your humid breath cold
one August night
and you fell down

through star poked clouds
to softly land on ankle high green
forever lost
cosmic corvine.

~

Before the fall
you took command of every branch
as bristled heads bobbed and bowed

*Nancy King Schofield*

in abeyance

midnight raids
and practiced flight for eggs
and gold and silver things
were booty for your renegades

who snapped them up
and stashed them
with all the rotten fishy bits
and pretty maids.

~

Now you lie broken black
and styrofoam blue
alien moving through
foreign space
salvaged hawk morsel

with proud glistening head
and predatory beak
hanging necklace loose
on downy breast

that drills into softness
with each rhythmic step
left right left right
my raven bobble head doll

refrigerated carcass slept
in frozen dream on ice cube pillow
and bed of peas
solitary seven day lockdown

your flight aborted
when air became so thick
you couldn't draw it in
and the sky startled

with clouds of promise
shattered into fragments
scattering reflected images
of your own Golgotha.

"Scratch a lover, and find a foe."
                        - Dorothy Parker

## Lullaby For Frozen Lovers

He's my Neruda man
but he's been
put on ice to cool
Delilah bled his
wasted heart
and sheared seven
glistening locks
that fell
on Anana's pale feet

then he grinded
grain like Samson
in a house that couldn't
hold him
his beauty was so fierce
before I locked him up
that's what I told him

an archer trained
to always hit the mark
with arrows velvet tipped
he won it all
and every heart was game
like my unsuspecting prey
fool  to every hidden treachery

each day I played my music
tentative fingers searching
notes on ivory keys
numbered like the hours
of my longing
but quickly dropped the bar
each time I heard
my name

irresistible collector
of broken lives
woven thick
with loneliness
and discontent
hopping restless
from lily pad
to unsuspecting lily
spinning
wordy strands
that kept each one
stuck in place

la la lover

yesterday
angry women
whipped their horses
searching for you
something
that you left behind
but they found nothing

witches' wage was paid
gold for spells
potions stirred
to bring you back
but there was nothing
though they waited
past a harvest rot

when horses fell
their wounds were bound
with citronella
honey
from the belly of a lion
you were that carcass full of bees

la la lover
lulls and lists

on tongues that lie
in streets and holy places
broken bones of Jesuits
roll until they turn to dust
while jackals
watch from crowded lairs
with hungry jaws
salivating
and children play in shadow
unaware

charisma kept a strangle
hold on girls that lied
while kissing
all your dimpled bits
those lusty daughters
lured you in with
oysters plump and
cups of gin
then they waited
while you melted
on their metal beds

now they know
your eyes of icy blue
were never true
and so they sing

la la lover.

## My Holy White Girls

I'm seated upright
back straight
limbs fused wooden
haphazard line
like chairs along the wall

skin resists rungs
that print their mark on flesh
an edition on bent vertebrae
and sloped shoulders
hardwood covers space
between expandable ribs
hugs bodies
cartilaginous

relics with cataracts
fill the room
waiting shucked mollusks
with human mouths
struck dumb
other parts not moving

a medical time mishap
of borrowed bodies
and disconnected dendrites
unresponsive
to neural synapse

nothing moves
except a sliver of silver
on Indian cotton
rising and falling
with each respiration
shallow and irregular
I view it from a distance
benign like beige
the colour of waiting
and these walls

avoiding all eye contact
to maintain composure
we stare our shared destiny
passive and solitary
every quarter hour
the list keeper arrives
punctually efficient
and calls a name
to enter the theatre
for the laser procedure

subtle rhythms
repetitive and monotonous
control the room
as we move in and out
one by one
programmed robots
performing unscripted parts
in the round
a film in slow motion

she calls my name
and I follow
wearing an expression
of indifference
another skill learned
to alleviate fear
and give comfort
taught by nursing sisters
swishing soundless
through antiseptic halls
years I spent with girls
of holy habit
my holy white girls.

## Skiff Lake Myth

Early morning lake rose
vaporous grey
undulating layers of
translucence
like just another day

I watched it melt hubbub
on birds
and overcrowded skies
splintered black
with feathered shrieking
the sound was a symphony
of panornithic mayhem

it punched landscape
and my senses with fists
both fell flat choking on silence
spellbound
as beams bounced zigzag
over cold stone
my toes squeezed
moist sponge of boards
wave lapped saturated

pale flesh mirrored
in the lake
hung disconnected
limbs raised to dive
rippled dissected

amphibian arched reluctant
to enter murky shallows
a stared liquid trapping house
with creature claws
and jaws that hiss


sacred keeper of the myth

a love story lost
beneath the waves
Titian around her face
before she disappeared
without a trace

when storms raged angry
tearing knotted limbs
a figure stalked the shore
mourning cries
battered folk with fright
awake all night

loons in love laughed
as sorrow wrapped the shore
in ribbons
poking holes in boats
and unsuspecting bathers

the lake hearing the call
rushed in to plug them up
and they sank to its rocky bed
things of lead.

"The only sin is the sin of being born."
                    - Samuel Beckett

## The Arrival

Before your arrival
eager men waited
spectacles and stethoscopes
lined up
restless birds I thought
strung on a wire
body language stiff
eyes darting
to avert mine
as they gathered
near the wall
croaking softly
birds beggin bread
beyond cold stirrups

supine captive
held tight
in stainless steel
I dreamed of leaving
sliding through tiled walls
into darkness
or resting my crate
on a shelf  with sutures
and cold
surgical instruments
an escape of fantasy
from the task at hand
successful retreat
from those
injecting medicinal
silence
to insure my limbs
stay frozen

suddenly

slicing through the mist
and other dilemma
was good nurse Mary
butterfly fingers
snipping and tying
stinging with needles
and ministering
salves and herbs
concocted like memories
for healing
while her white feet
ran circles
of reassurance
to erase my fear
and chanting
melodic notes in my ear
as she passed


meanwhile
the theatre chief
paced like a Viking
back from a raid
bristling impatience
rained on his groupies
white faced and young
as milk bubbles
rose
from their throat
I watched them
float to the ceiling
like circles of hope
then burst overhead

finally nurse Mary
moving so quickly
was creating an uproar
polishing instruments
and chopping catgut
with lightening speed

causing the bears
to lumber off
and the birds and archangels
to fly out the window

no one was left
to receive the blue
pumpkin baby
hanging precarious
from his umbilical vine
except for me
pushing you outward
breathing in light
and seeing
when I looked past
the trays
windows and tubing
into the future
what I had always
dreamed in the past.

## There Were So Many

Sometimes we sat
around it
beating spoon or finger
rhythms
cacophonic
machine gun notes
fired through thick warmth
of summer
forced quiet overboard
we beat it till our hands tingled

a table on the east porch
hidden blue in shadow
felt cold to the touch
like people sometimes
I remember it white
the color of death
or slick boiled icing
piled high and glossy
sometimes we sat around it

in sprawling August heat
we watched magic begin
"fairies are here" said Alex
as emerald hummers
flashed scarlet
laser diving
sweet sticky liquid
to make them stay
perched
above  our madding world
ignoring us
looking the other way

chairs facing the road
gave us front row seats
as sun threw purple
on porcelain plates

light splashed bottle green
through privileged space
with spruce and pine
sentries of a hundred lives

umbrellas marched
marking time with coolers
hung from terry cloth arms
as beach bunnies
fled the tide
bouncing babies
on hips
in wind filled bonnets
there were so many.

"If you take the earth as a whole,
 eventually there's nowhere to move on to."
                        - Clive Anderson

## Unravelling

Threads
holding the seams
of the village together
were unraveling

what began
as a whisper
of increased maladies
and general mayhem
soon became shouted
out
complaints
of pestilence
and failed crops

increasing famine
and disease
sent fear racing rampant
through the people
spinners stopped treadles
spinning
wool
for drafty tunics
where sheep grazed
burghers shook fists
at the heavens
vowing never to return
until there was order

in the beginning
such phenomena
might have slipped by
unnoticed
but for the seamstress

with mystical knowledge
of blood and bone
who cured fever
with herbs
rhymes
and stones
breathed life back
into babies
cold blue
mothers bled red

with anxious eyes
and teeth clacking
in time with her busy feet
she circled
the village perimeter
dousing fires day and night
and making repairs
along the edges
with little
for restoration
except a tiny thimble
of hope
worn bare

hair smoking black
and white
singed by sparks
spiraling
she stopped
looked down
at her hands
the color of charcoal
and examined long
boney fingers
black and bruised
immobile
the colour of failure

stunned

by such revelation
she stopped
to face the bad news
and leave
stepping carefully
over carcasses that glowed
scarlit coals
that lit her way
dying embers she thought
on a hearth of sadness

soon the soldiers
would return
from the Great Campaign
battle worn
wounded
searching lost love
and other things
they left behind

but they would find nothing

and the infirmed
who needed herbal cure
blood from beasts
for broth
to treat chronic
tribulations

would weaken and be gone

seeing darkness
looming
in the future
she ran to warn the elders
powerful as gods
hoping they would listen
but instead
they laughed
huddled around a fire

spitting tobacco missiles
into dancing flames
and while they laughed
and spit
the world
as they knew it
went down the drain.

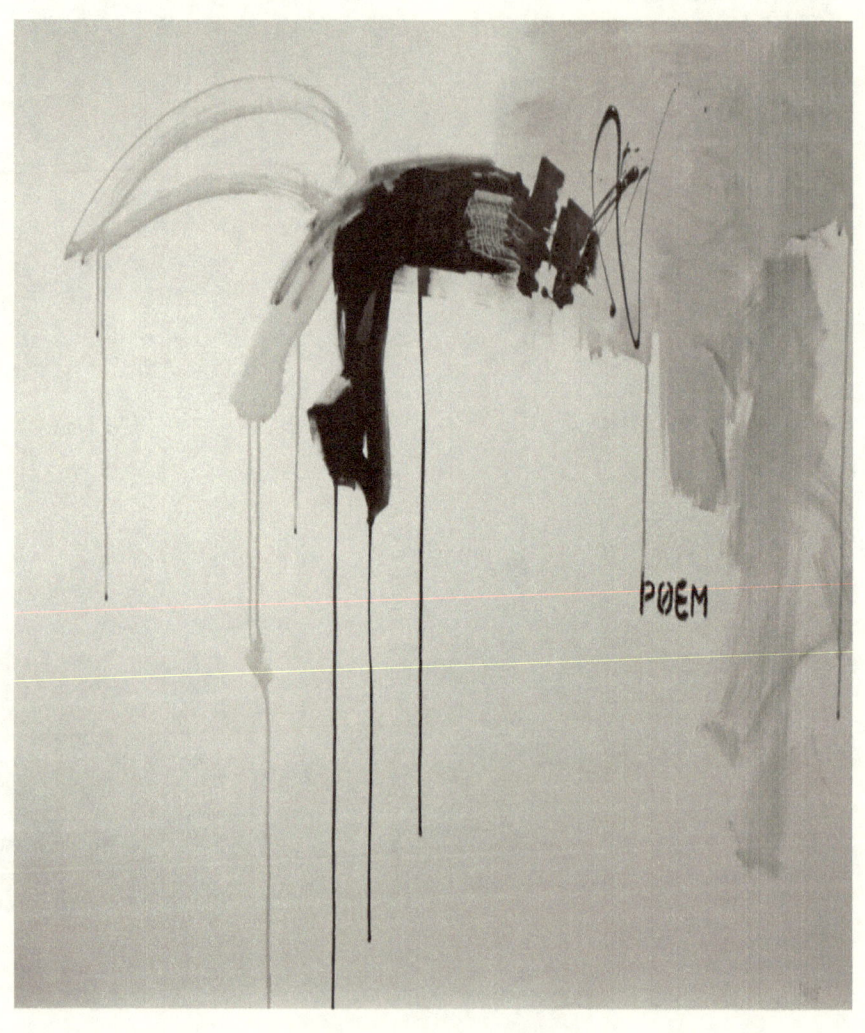

*Poem, David Skyrie, 2011*

# David Skyrie

## *Poems from South America*

### La Recoletta

The doors are open.
The guard dog sleeps.
It is so easy to walk
Into the City of the Dead.

An old man sketches.
A young girl weeps.
Scales are falling from the angels
In the City of the Dead.

The air is heavy.
The wild vine creeps
Across the marble houses
In the City of the Dead.

The sun shines hard.
We walk the narrow streets.
My love says, "I can smell it."
In the City of the Dead.

We cross the park.
Only a patch of grass keeps
Us from the City of the Dead.
The doors are open.

*Buenos Aires, 1999*

*David Skyrie*

## Here in Paradise

The streets are cobblestone
And the trees are blue
And everything is so nice
Where I live here in paradise.

The little white houses
Are lined with palms
And the gates that circle them
Are topped with shards of glass
And sometimes from a distance
In the afternoon sun
It all shines like ice
Where I live here in paradise.

The dogs have eaten
All of the cats and the horses
That pull the carts of garbage
Are all stuck in traffic with the fumes
And the stench and the air
So bad it burns their eyes
Where I live here in paradise.

The shoeless mothers
Cry in the streets
And the children sleep
On the sidewalks like angels
Wearing rags and haloes of flies
Where I live here in paradise.

I wonder where it was we learned
And who it was that taught us
That we are not supposed to care?
Slowly I unlearn and slowly I break down
Because it's all right there before me
And I can see it with my eyes
Where I live here in paradise.

*Porto Alegre, Brazil, April 20, 1999*

## She Holds Me

She holds me,
this poetry,
like the newly
arrived prisoner
under the
hard hoses
of humility.

She washes
from me
the arrogance
and the pride.

She offers
me silence
and a great
poverty
to help me
serve my time.

I dance
like a fool
in my cell.

*Porto Alegre, Brazil, 1999*

"There is a crack in everything.
That's how the light gets in."
            - Leonard Cohen

## If She Were Perfect

*After a poem by Vinicius de Moraes,*
*"Receita De Mulher" ("Woman Recipe")*

If she were perfect
this other woman of mine
whenever I called her down
she would come quickly
appearing  instantly
not a micro-second of hesitation
and just as quickly she would go
as when walking in a forest
and after a twig snaps underfoot
a bird might take to the air
in a blizzard of feathers
and become suddenly gone
out of the corner of one's eye
before one even realizes a bird
was there and one is left only with
a heavy foot, a silent forest and
the absence of a bird perhaps
only the memory of a bird and
she would come and go
as quickly as that
but she does not of course.
 And if she were perfect
this other woman of mine
how silently she would
seem to float towards me
like a Geisha in an opera
not a limb moving
but her whole being moving
as if on wheels invisible
moving towards me moving
me to poetry and her hair
would be auburn-red-blonde-jet-

black and straight with curls
that were close-cropped and
stretched halfway down her back
and across her eyes, her eyes
the colour of sand in moonlight
eyes that call to you
and say "Come!" and "Stay!"
at the same time eyes
that recall a perfect verse
by a favoured and dead poet
eyes of a woman
capable of holding
without the slightest effort
a thousand-and-one
degrees of silence
and a mouth like a poem
that is perfect with lips
that are wet and red and
as guilty as wine spilled
on a pale carpet or
as tragic as blood clotted
on a bathroom tissue and
such would be her lips that
men would dare no
further comparisons
but simply fall down and
weep in their lusting for her.
 And if she were perfect
this other woman of mine
oh if she were perfect
her  body would be
more round than straight
more full than empty
more flesh than bone
more real than imagined
a  body to fit so perfectly
across my own that
when we made love
the darkness would be
a seamless cover

a perfect blackness
across our polished bed
with not the smallest crack
between us to let the moonlight
shine through.
 And if she were perfect
this other woman of mine
there would be the necessity
for beauty without compromise
a real beauty that is
final and pure and shining
but most of all resplendent
in its innumerable
imperfections.

*Porto Alegre, Brazil,1999*

**Expat**

Are the leaves falling
back home now?
Are the other Leafs winning?

Has anyone answered
the French question yet?

Its been a year now
without winter and
I find I am actually
recalling the snow
craving it like a junkie
the cold
and the white
and the wind
and the blackouts
and the weather warnings
and the stay off the roads tonight
and the drifting of it all
over the fence lines
and in the barns
the water buckets
frozen solid
and the soggy wet
woollen smell
of mittens drying
by the wood stove
and outside the temperature
                              drops
so low that you need
a second thermometer
just to record it
                    drops
so low that it remains indescribable
to my Brazilian friends
here in this land
of blue leaves and summer
that just goes on and on and on.

*David Skyrie*

Here the heat is making us crazy.
And far too passionate.
We fear we can no longer
be called Canadian.

*Porto Alegre, Brazil, 1999*

## Several Cranes in the Blue Air

A man in his mind
walks up a mountain-side in Japan.
When he reaches the top he knows the air
will be cool and good and there will be a rock
upon which he will be able to sit and look
down into the valley where the wooden bridge
will seem but a twig, the temple a crane's egg.

The man has never been to Japan.
In fact, the man has never been out of Montreal.
The man is old and thin and has worked
all his days for the same company.
Five days a week, nine hours a day
the man is a packer, packing
imported giftware, trinkets, into cardboard cartons.
He seals the cartons with gummy tape,
slaps a label on, sends them down a roller
to the shipper.
The man does not hate his job.

Sometimes he steals.
Mails a box or two to his brother's house.
Sells the junk in taverns.

The day that marked his twenty-fifth year
with the company, the president came to see him.
Offered him a gold watch and a free lunch at Ruby Foo's.
The man accepted the watch, declined the lunch.
Told the president that in twenty-five years
not once had he been late getting back from lunch.
By God, he wasn't going to start now.

The man enjoys packing the Japanese items.
One item intrigues him. A fine ink drawing
rolled into a scroll. Unfurled, it shows
a man leading a donkey up a mountain-side.
The mountain is capped with snow.
In the foreground is a temple.

To the right, a wooden foot-bridge.
Several cranes are in the blue air.


On the job, the man brags about his son.
His son works for a soft-drink company.
Sits in front of a moving belt watching
bottles go around and around all day.
The man would like a job like that.
A sit-down job. The man has bad feet.


Rice-paper. Rice-paper.
Sometimes the man has a lot to drink
and wants to write letters to his friends.
Write them all on rice-paper.
He never does though.
His bottom dresser drawer is filled with rice-paper.
His wife keeps threatening to throw it all out.

He met a Japanese man once.
A salesman from Tokyo. The president
Was showing him around the shop.
He had cold eyes and wore a blue blazer.
His neck had wrinkles at the spot where his tie
was tied on too tightly. Not at all like the man
In the scroll who wore a flowing robe and whose eyes
though hidden, could only be soft.

Soon the man will be retired.
He is not afraid of all of the time
he will have to do nothing.
He can always go to Japan.

In the foreground there will be a temple.
Several cranes will be in the blue, blue air.

## So Much Coal to Squeeze
### (A Song Perhaps)

It sure ain't easy
With you so far away
Are you as lonely
As I am today.

Alone in this oasis
Tapping away on this machine
Trying to pour my love
Onto this tiny little screen.

I can't even touch you
And that's what hurts
There are too many miles
But I guess it could be worse.

I feel so alone
I feel like a fool
I feel like a teacher
But nobody's in school.

The walls are thin
I can hear the neighbor's moan
Her headboard is rocking
While I lie silent and alone.

I'm thinking of you
I'm trying to behave
It's hard to face the mirror
So I don't even shave.

I've sang for a few suppers
I've kissed a few rings before
But since your heart joined mine
Well I don't do that any more.

I'm doing the dishes
I'm holding onto the dream

*David Skyrie*

I'm working on the novel
I'm keeping the bathroom clean

I'm working on a diamond
There's so much coal to squeeze
And such a mountain of words
Before my tiny soul can be pleased.

I'm listening to Mclaren
To Leonard and to Waits
I'm getting' behind my mule
I've learned a little from old mistakes.

If I could stretch my arm
Reach over the continents
Across America and Mexico
Then this might make sense.

My time will come
My words be read
My spirit at peace
When all is said.

And when all is said
And when all is done
Together we will shine
Like diamonds in the sun.

*Oasis Park Chalets, Shediac, N.B.*

## Jonathan Swift Drinking

Jonathan sits
in the local inn
downing a few

& decides that
yes indeedy
chivalry is dead.

The word gets out
& a flurry of
English gentlemen
fly underground.

Jonathan belches
& leaves.

*David Skyrie*

**Poetry or Truth**

Like Layton
he writes about
fucking & raging-
      but his wife
      is getting tired
      of reading about it.

## For My Son As Yet Unborn

1.
A part of me
grows in you.

Like grass
in winter,
unseen
the child grows
inside of you.

Inside of you
he eats of you
to be of you
an extension of you
part me/part you
in time to come
apart from us
an extension
of our time
for a time
only.

A part of me
grows in you.
Our lives shall be re-
arranged.


2.
We made love last night
and I stroked the tight
curve of hardness
that is you

(wondering all the while
if you would praise me
for the gift of life
or curse me forever

for starting another private race
against Old Man Bones.)


3.
Should you grow tired, my son,
of trying to interpret
the thousand and one
degrees of silence
a woman can hold
in her eyes,
persist,

for I could
not.


4.
And will my words be wise enough
to keep him from danger, from ruin?
Will my heart be strong enough
to let him roam?

Will my blood run precious
in his veins as my father's blood
runs precious in mine?

Will it be raining on the day
he chooses to leave us
and will the pain match the imagined pain?

And will he dance
on my grave
or will I cry
over his?

God only knows
and He's not telling.

5.
Because the baby is coming the sun is warm.

Because the baby is coming the geese fly
high and safe above the crouching hunters.

Because the baby is coming God is in his world.

Because the baby is coming I make love to your breasts.

Because the baby is coming I take over the cleaning of the cat's filthy
box.


6.
The snow falls quietly
in Williamsburg tonight
and the haloed moon lights
my way to the barn for free.
Inside, the animals are fine.
Rabbits snuggle in straw,
ducks walk about duck-like
quacking their annoyance
at my intrusion.
An old hen sits passive
on four smooth eggs
and atop several bales of hay
three cats are sleeping impervious
to all but the noisiest of mice.

If memory serves me well,
it was on a night similar to this
that you were conceived
(with quiet snow and peace in a small
corner of the planet);
                        though the image of you,
the desire for you has always been
in my mind, in my father's mind
and in his father's before him
stretching back in time like

*David Skyrie*

an eternal calendar, a contract
of flesh, blood and thought
through the wild centuries

## Among Other Things
### *For Al Purdy*

*"Imagine, a grown man writing this crap!"*
you said to me in a letter and I thought
as a matter of fact before you arrived
Canadian poetry could be likened
to hard stools crapped out in pain
by foppy Englishmen but I begin to digress
and must get back to the more specific crap
you mentioned and your question
as to why we write it and to tell you the truth Al,
just the thought of you asking was enough to scare me
because if you didn't know, then who did?
But of course you did know,
and the reasons are indeed many
but you wanted the newer guys
to find out for themselves because
if they couldn't then they shouldn't
be writing, right? And as for encouragement
you wrote back offering among other things,
*"I don't like young poets. I see too damn much of them!"*
and among other things still *"let your mind go off,
hence your poems in a million directions"*
and I did and found the many answers to be
that we write it because we strive for beauty
and all that leads to it and damn the days
when just the thought of it hurts and
we write it because poetry is an argument
we must have with ourselves
and you have had thousands Al
and haven't lost one yet and
we write it because we need
the attention and we need
to be remembered and
we can think of nothing better
to do, literally, and  better still,
among other things, we write it because
there are so many other things, big and small
that need to be written down

to be documented and spoken
things among other things
like the names of New Brunswick towns
that trip and stumble in your mouth
with a poetry all to themselves, towns
like Haute Aboujagane or Kouchibouguac
or Memramcook where the graves look out
over the green Acadian valleys, or among other things
like the way Winter hangs around here
into early May like a tired old guest and the snow
flies stubborn against the jackpine and the budding alder trees
or among other remembered things
like once how the Northern Harrier Hawk
lay cradled in my wife's arms dying
and how his neck seemed no longer able to support
his head but he kept raising it and it kept falling
and once when he looked at me I swear I saw
through the foggy clouds in his eyes and
as if in a movie starring myself
I saw the marshland open up to me
from a great height and I flew around
and around it in ever-shortening circles and
I glided lower and silently closer, closer
to the ground zeroing in on a skittering field mouse
running in panic for his life and I swear
I felt my talons opening but I digress
again see how the mind just goes
off in a million directions
and I thank you for it
resting in your grave
or tripping through the universe
fantastic or among other things
I thank you for all of it.

## *New poems*

### Lie

After covering
Sex & death
The poet turns
His gaze towards
God .

Here,
Volumes
Lie.

*David Skyrie*

## An Old Soldier

An old soldier
In the sacred parade
My father sang
As he marched.

Ever the good son
I said my Hail Mary's
My many mea culpa's
And I followed
Carrying the cross.

I covered the statues
With the black velvet cloth
Snuffed out the candles
And laid me down to sleep.

Awakened I begin
My own walk
Out of the incense
Towards my future.

## God Is an American

Whether he speaks English or French,
Whether god is a man or a woman,
It's all so academic now.
Now that he is dead.

I believe Camus
Perhaps Nietzsche,
To be responsible.

**Angel Drift**

And just
As the angels
Above us

Drift &
Linger

At their
Various
Levels

We too
Linger &

Drift

Towards
Our own
Un-
Paralleled

Catastrophes

Joys

## Heaven

Some
Restrictions
Apply.

*Flight of Fancy, Elaine Amyot, 2012*

# Lee D. Thompson

## Hairball Man

### I

Oh God, it was still hanging on.

Only two days earlier she had thrown it in the trash but this morning *what was it doing on the kitchen floor*? The floor was cold and blue and it, whatever it was, was black and a mess and how could it have gotten there? She didn't have any children nor any pets and no lovers to speak of so *what the*, she said aloud, when she entered the kitchen. *What the?* Did the garbage pail fall over and somehow right itself and replace itself back under the sink and shut the doors behind it? Or did she do that in her sleep during the night? But she didn't sleepwalk, so there must have been a better explanation than that. Some law of physics, perhaps, some law that allowed wet things to slide out of garbage pails and strand themselves on cold kitchen floors. Heat, yes – composting heat got the thing going sliding up the plastic pail slipping under the doors but once on the floor the cold took the movement from it. But that's ridiculous.

It had small hands that were gripping her, causing shivers of fear and disgust to ooze down her spine and into the soles of her feet. And then she started to scream and when she did start to scream she could have sworn it held on tighter. Her scream intensified and she didn't know why, it wasn't that big a thing no bigger than a rat but a rat, she would have screamed had a rat been attached to her hand. Her scream sounded like a rising siren but it was human, too, of course, and was *it*, too, of course? A rising siren that she couldn't stop and if that wasn't bad enough good God, it looked at her. It had eyes, dark eyes that blinked, and so the screaming continued for a while.

*It's only a bruise*, he told her. *I think you'll be alright. That's such a long way to fall. Tell me, what do you think of marriage? No, no... don't sit up, Madam, lay here a while. It's a glorious morning, is it not?*

There was a wet cloth on her forehead, and it was soothing. Her head ached so much right now and she didn't know what time of day it was. That was a panic, like sleeping in the afternoon and waking and thinking it's morning but no, it's not. And what were dreams, really, letters wanting to be numbers and he spoke again, said *can I get you something? some tea? or maybe a neck massage? here just let me...*

His voice was soft, controlled, had a touch of a lisp. He was very polite. Oh God, she said, there was something in my kitchen, or wait, no, she didn't say that, she thought that, yes, kept it in because she didn't know what was what. She breathed and felt the wet cloth shift a little, she raised her hand to replace it on her forehead but it seemed to shift back of its own volition, meaning: the cloth moved before she touched it. Something's not right, she said, but no, she didn't say that either. When you're ready, I'll help you, he said. Just give me your hand and we'll be certain no one topples again.

That was sweet of him.

But it wasn't him.

And now he, it, *whatever the hell was happening,* she had reacted to the shifting and the little hands that held an eyebrow and things connected, H became 9, and boy did she scream again, shook and stood and with a movement that was like erasing her forehead swiped across and it flew, landed with a wet smack against the kitchen window and then slid slowly down.

*What the hell?* she said, truly shouting. She looked for something, a broom, a knife...

Then *it* said...

But wait, what was it? It was moving on the windowsill now and yesterday no, two days ago she had thrown it into the trash, had pulled it out it was so disgusting, she had gagged and had flung it into the trash. It was speaking, it was saying oh dear in such a sad, shocked voice and moving on the windowsill on hands and knees and screaming seemed to be the only thing to do right now, an act of defiance against something that had crawled up inside her and stuck there, she swore, she swore she had thrown it into the trash, had yanked it out but....

Then it stood...

I'm okay, it said, its voice soft, shaken, and: apologies if I startled you. This wasn't my intention but sometimes, I must admit, people do have this reaction to me – startled, a touch nonplussed even. Why, I've almost come to expect it. It extended a hand.

May I introduce myself?

No! she shouted. No! God! Get out! Its hands were like spiders, like black widows, they would crawl over her at night and she looked about and found the broom and threw it and although he ducked, cowered on the ledge, she missed by a mile, the broom rattled in a far corner. So she grabbed a frying pan and ran with it raised over her head and she would do it, she would end this now and when she opened her eyes it would be over, you had to smash these things out of your life and hopefully not break anything else in the process, but that's not how it happened, it wasn't supposed to say wait, wait Madam, and she wasn't supposed to open an eye and see it pleading its little hands waving the looming frying away and for a moment she felt a tenderness, a female urge to mother, perhaps, though nothing like this had ever suckled at a woman's breast and when it smiled, flashed its black teeth, the pan came down fast. I'm sorry, I'm sorry! she said, but she kept slamming the frying pan down.

I don't know how long I was in there, Madam, I really couldn't tell you. Time slows when it's like that. I dream, yes I do, often of flying, and of swimming. I dream I'm a butterfly, but also a manta ray, and the sea is full of sunlight, so it's not so bad. But thank you for pulling me out. I don't know why it has to be like that.

She didn't know what it was, that's what she should have asked first. Not what the hell were you doing in there, in the drainpipe, the other day, but *what are you? Why are you? How is this possible?* Those were questions that should have followed. And what time of day was it?

She was backed into a corner in the kitchen, sitting on the broomstick, her fingers pulling at the broom's fibers. Her hands were trembling, her wrists sore. She had watched it, had watched it *peel itself* from the underside of the frying pan, like a mirage of hair and heat it lifted slowly and seemed to brushed itself off, take a deep breath, and approach her. It was speaking, going on about how the world is full of mistakes and slippery elements of existence and it sounded a bit insane really, though after having taken such a pounding who could blame it? Or blame him. Its voice was male and much too close. There was more panic when she thought two days ago I pulled you from the drainpipe and I wondered why there was so much hair in the kitchen sink. Oh god yes I reached in with two slender fingers and pulled what looked like a little head and at first just a fleeting thought I thought there was a doll in drainpipe but of course it was just long black hair and grease and bits and pieces of bread and pasta and who knows what else. You came out so easily and I remember feeling elated, yes, joyous that I didn't have to pull or really dig down there or take the pipes apart and I loved this kitchen and I think I was laughing when I dropped you in the wet trash under the kitchen sink. Why would I be laughing having just pulled such a disgusting thing from a drainpipe? I don't know why but I was laughing, couldn't stop laughing and the days went on, I called Kelly and told her that I felt like a new woman that some change had come over me some release had occurred and maybe I would leave this all behind, sell the house and travel. But then this morning humming in my bathrobe there you were, on the cold floor, moving, moving, what were you doing on the cold floor in my kitchen why are you here go away go away!

She kicked it at, but with little conviction, for her feet were bare. She pulled herself to herself arms and legs cradled closely so what was it doing on her lap now? what was it doing nuzzled on her hipbone? how did it manage to hold her still while it crawled up her shirt and kissed her neck, kissed her cheek and whispered it's alright Madam, you haven't hurt me much. I've been through worse, I truly have. May I rest here a while? You have such an exquisite collarbone. My heart is racing from this stress, but yours is too. I think we should move to the bedroom, Madam, it's not very comfortable here. Your bed is soft and welcoming, the light through the trees falls in gently, we could cuddle, tell stories, recall past loves, our families, childhood friends who were cruel to us, old men who fed us candy, the dog down the street, the one that limped, that was missing an ear. We could sing songs, even. *Tra-la-la la-la-la...*

## II

Oh dear, there's a spider above the kitchen sink. I don't know how to kill it. What's the best way to kill a spider? Sprays in the kitchen aren't a good idea, I know. A broom? No, it'll only hang on, the web will get caught on the broom, the spider will swing around and around and then it'll be in my hair, wrapped around my head. How do they get in here? Flies? The trash beneath the sink, yes, flies. Do you think it will die soon? How long do they live for? Ugh, but then it'll fall into the sink and it'll twitch when the water pours over it! No, that's not funny! Stop laughing! You know I hate them! What? Oh, I'm doing fine, couldn't be better. What? A man? No, no, there's no... no, there's no... Haha, well maybe I'm going to keep him all to myself! No, no, there's no man, there's... Why do you think I'm lying? You can hear me smiling? Kelly! Stop that! Wait... wait... Um... at the grocery store... last month... yes... haha... not telling! No! Not telling! Tell me how to get rid of the spider! What? Oh, he's scared of them too, more than I am, actually. I know, big man scared of a bug. Tall? You know, average, maybe a little less... no, not blond, dark... eyes dark... sure, yes, sexy voice... tender hands... well... he's away right now, work related... and... what I love most is how we laugh in bed, Kelly, how he gathers me in his arms and twirls me about then sets me gently on the bed and begins to undress me so slowly, oh it's torture, I have to *beg* him to just rip them all off and take me quickly, it's as if he can read my mind, knows exactly what I'm wanting when I want it and he lights candles gives massage better than any man I've ever known and he's such a wonderful cook. So many dishes. We eat everything in bed. We never leave the bed. We stay in the tangled sheets all day. We lay in each other's arms. We caress. We sleep. We dream. She didn't know where it was. The phone was hanging at her side and it had been there, in the window, moving oily slow behind the sheer curtain the hot green garden behind him and she had been keeping an eye on him but lost him. Where are you? She hissed it. *Where are you you little fucker!* Oh, it was so unnerving, it was so weird that way. Where would it curl up next? Her shoes! Always in her shoes... pulled it out by the foot last time and that *ugh squishy against her toes* she hated it, hated it but then night would come he would slip under the covers and the tension would be gone. How could she explain *that*? God it came slipping up her thighs wet and slick and you'd think she could scream or jump out of bed certainly could were it a drenched mouse but she couldn't move, maybe because she knew where it was headed? Because oh she knew where it was headed and she was so ashamed but her thighs would open wide and she would claw at the sheets and throw her head back and he wasn't even close yet God how do you explain this? How do you tell your girlfriend this? My legs tremble for hours, I giggle, I call him the filthiest things but can he leave? will my thighs let him slip away? I spend all day pining for night and today I bought a blindfold and black curtains, no, no I cannot see him, I close my eyes, I just feel, I just sense, *I am hiding in your shoes again, Madam, please come and get me, nobody knows where I am. Come, come and get me... come find me...*

### III

She was screaming in the kitchen again. You can't follow me like that! You can't! You scared the hell out of me you little bastard! I need to do some things alone, alright? And I don't need to be freaking out at the drugstore with everyone watching me. And I don't need to be scared to open my purse wondering if you're hiding in there. Don't *do* that!

But Madam, he said, I wanted to surprise you, to make you smile. I love your smile, Madam.

She was pacing the kitchen, furious, wanting to pull her hair but sometimes just touching her hair gave her the creeps and he kept saying he was sorry, terribly sorry, it's a tragic mistake, just tragic, and how in the world did he get flowers? How in the world did he pay for flowers? Three bouquets were resting on the kitchen counter, splendid arrangements, a hundred little hearts were drawn on each card, so how was she supposed to stay mad at him? No, she had to stay firm, but he had such a way of making her feel guilty and... lacking... but he was such a better partner than she was, really, always upbeat, tender, loving, you're a real moody Judy, he'd say, perhaps we should go on vacation? Yes, we could fly to Mexico, or Spain...

I merely called them, Madam, he said, and when they arrived I left the money on the table. I'm in the basement, I shouted, please put the flowers on the counter. Of course, I was hiding under the table. Clever of me, right?

Don't *do* that! They'll find you... and....

I'm sorry, Madam... don't you like them?

They're beautiful.

She was crying now, sitting on the floor and weeping. She couldn't explain why she was weeping but he came over and climbed up her sleeve, sat on her shoulder and caressed her neck and nibbled her earlobes, all of which only made her cry more. What was she supposed to do? She didn't know what she was supposed to do anymore. I hate my job, she told him, they're pressuring me all the time, maybe I need to make changes. He kept nibbling her ear, she could feel his prickly erection against her jugular and it made her shiver, her skin pucker. Stop, she said, stop, then wait, there was the top of a head in the window, someone was coming to the back door, she frantically stood, grabbed her lover, slapped him into trash under the sink and flattened her clothing and got the door. Oh Kelly, she said, what a surprise... no, no, I'm fine... really, no, I haven't been crying... just, chopping onions. Oh, let me help, said Kelly. And so they made a stew, laughing and chopping and soon he was buried beneath the choppings of everything that went in the stew and it was only later, in the evening, that she said she was sorry. She was washing the coffee grounds from his body and she'd never washed him before, and he squirmed a lot, but she found she could pull out the macaroni and lint and gunk and some of the gaggy other things that had collected between his fibers and soon he was shiny. He smiled blackly. The soup smelled wonderful, he said, I would very much like meet Kelly, and she started to cry again. That night she dreamed she ripped him to pieces, while washing him. It was hard to believe how much blood filled the bathtub.

# IV

They flew to Spain. It was the craziest thing to do, she knew, and she couldn't afford it, but everyone had thought it a wonderful idea. She hadn't been herself of late, it would do her good. During the flight, as she watched the distant ocean sparkling, he stayed on her inner thigh, strapped to her garter. From time to time he'd reach up and slip her panties aside and caress her, mischievous devil, and she'd try to keep her face calm, or hide it in a magazine. The bald man beside her seemed annoyed by her fidgeting, so she'd squeeze her thighs together until he stopped moving down there.

They had argued about how he should travel, and she'd wanted to put him in the luggage, but he said he might freeze, or a sniffer dog might find him, and she said stay still pretend you're a doll for chrisakes, you've been through worse, but in the end he won.

He always won.

They all knew what was going on, didn't they? They all knew she was sick, that she liked it. Whispers were crawling up and down the aisles, they knew what was going on. Show us, they would say, show us what's up your snatch. Let us see that hairy thing. She stood and rushed to the washroom, sat on the toilet, reached down and set him on her lap. Thank you, Madam, he said, it was getting a little muggy down there. Not that I mind, but it is good to see your face. I love your face. He lay back, head resting on one arm, watching her, smiling. She peed, realizing she couldn't do it, couldn't do what she was sure she was going to do while rushing up the aisle. Her legs were shaking. The sound of the toilet's mile-high vacuum flush was harsh, but he remained in her hand. And that was something.

# V

No, Kelly, it was terrible. It rained the whole time! Started off with a drizzle and by the day we left, I swear, it was a monsoon. Six days of rain, in Spain. No, no, it was a good idea, don't apologize. We're just... going through something right now. I'm trying to be big about it, but some of his habits... they annoy me, Kelly. She looked around and couldn't see him, and you know what, she didn't care either, let him listen, the little creep, maybe he'd learn a thing or two. Oh, he's just... he's very clingy, and he tries to make me feel guilty about everything. He's sweet about it but... What? No, even that's... dried up. Haha. I know, I know. God, in Spain, he just wouldn't stop! Not now, I'd tell him, I don't feel good, but Madam, he'd say, I... Oh. Um. Madam, yes... he likes to call me that. Yeah, he's... weird that way. You know, polite but...well he spent a lot of time in London, when he was little. He's different, but an angel sometimes, and.... She shouted, dropped the phone. I told you not to do that! she shouted. She threw a shoe at him, then picked up the phone and raised the receiver and held it high but she breathed, could hear Kelly's tiny voice, said oh sorry, Kelly, no, everything's OK, he just... he... startled me, snuck up on me, you know how I hate that, Kelly, how my brothers did that when I was young, and my father too, everyone hiding in corners jumping out at me, it's why I'm frightened by everything now, I'm sorry... God, I'll have to call you back....

She threw the phonebook at him, called him a rat, chased him down the hallway and caught him before he slipped under a cabinet. She locked him in the washroom and slid a wet towel under the doorframe, so he wouldn't slip out. He was always slipping out of everything, everywhere. Damn. Madam, Madam, he cried, you are hurting me. Why do you want to hurt me? Let me out, you are only hurting yourself by hurting me. Please, Madam. I'll be good, Madam. Please. But she told him she wanted him to go, said it wasn't working anymore, they were just too... *incompatible*. It's been good, she said, really, but I think we should go our separate ways now.

He was quiet for a moment, no doubt gathering his thoughts, and she knew he'd find some way to wriggle out of this. She checked the doorframe, thought about the toilet, the sink, the pipes, wondered if that was what had happened, if some other woman had fallen for his charm, then grew weary of it, locked him in the bathroom and he escaped down a pipe, eventually worked his way into her place, her pipe. She shuddered. Or maybe he was watching me, stalking me, planned it all. Bastard. Did the door handle turn? Did the towel move just a little? Madam, she heard, can't we just talk a moment? You've been under so much stress of late and your decisions are not rational. How about we fill up the tub and lounge and laugh? A foot massage always does a world of good. She shuddered again, saw the towel twitch some more. I'll start doing that at this very moment, Madam. Yes, the water was running. Just go away, she said. Leave me alone, I moved here to find myself, I needed my space, so please leave, find someone else, another victim, I'm not your victim anymore. The water stopped running. She could hear splashing. It's ready now, Madam, please come and join me.

One night she dreamed he crawled into her ear, was in the back of her skull, moving down her spine. And one night she dreamed he lived in her mouth and when she spoke people could see him. The looks they gave her. And she dreamed he made her pregnant and there was a nest of him in her, like burdock, the doctor told her this, shaking his head. *Burdock.* She'd go into labour, likely wouldn't live through it, everything was mangled inside. They way he looked at her, that doctor, like she was sick.

You'd better leave, she said, menace in her voice.

Who? Me? What's going on?

Kelly! Kelly was standing in the kitchen, oh God. Oh, nothing, she said, but Kelly wouldn't believe that. There was splashing from the bathroom and oh no, Kelly'd see how sick she was too. She stood and said, nothing, nothing, Kelly, then pulled the towel from the bathroom door and said I was just running a bath. But isn't someone in there? Kelly said, and oh no, he's gone, she said, just the wind I guess, stirring the waters. Valerie, what the hell? Madam, she heard. Oh, the radio, she said, left it on! In the bathroom. She rushed in and shut the door and he was there, sitting in two inches of water, smiling, so she swooped down and grabbed the fucker, thought she'd flush him but Kelly was behind her, saying Val, please, what's going on? What're you holding behind your back? Nothing, nothing, she said, leaving the bathroom, spinning in the kitchen. There's no radio in here, Val. Oh you know, she said. That's all she said, oh, you know. Laughing. He was squirming so she held him tight, made like she was scratching her back, or adjusting her bra strap. Kelly was telling her she brought some food, some fresh fruit, you look so weak, Val, have you been eating? Are you depressed? Oh no, her face was breaking, she was starting to cry and Kelly, such a great friend, she hugged Val, arms wrapped around just above where she held him and shit, he almost slipped out, but she had him firmly by his head, his limbs flailing wildly. He bit her but she held on. Are you in pain, Val? She shook her head said no, no, she was fine, but she was crying and was blood dripping on the floor behind her? Shit, shit.

You need something good in you, Val, something to clean out your system, reenergize you. She nodded, wincing. She stood on the spots of blood. Kelly was unloading a cloth bag and out tumbled mangos and bananas and a pineapple. Fuck, he wouldn't stop biting her fucking thumb! Oh, honey, Kelly said, it'll be OK. It's him, isn't it? She nodded. He has to go, Honey. He really does. Kelly started to put the fruit in the food processor. Her famous smoothies. Kelly asked if there was any kiwi in her fridge, headed for the fridge and before she could even think, she'd leaped, she'd done it. The whir of the machine. Oh god. The mango and banana and pineapple the soft creamy yellow of it now clouded with clumps of black and she kept on holding the button down, hand shaking but she wouldn't stop she wasn't going to ever stop so Kelly unplugged the machine and said oh my fuck, Valery. I'm sorry. Shit. That must've been a bad mango. Gross. And before she could stop her, Kelly had poured it all down the sink.

## Her, a Story

Shelby was a man who had gone many years without making love, so when he woke early one Sunday morning with a woman by his side he should have been pleased. That he wasn't pleased, and was, in truth, distressed, can be explained by the fact that he had no recollection of how this woman came to be at his side. He had not gone to a party the evening before, and had not consumed any quantity of alcohol in the past year, nor had he taken drugs. His initial conclusion was that this woman had simply walked in and decided to sleep next to him, that perhaps she was confused, a mental patient, and had not taken her medication. How would she react when she woke to find *him*, a stranger, in her bed? He thought he had better get out of bed. For a moment he wondered if he knew her, but he didn't know anyone who looked like that.

Her hair was black, glossy, curling in at the ends. It wasn't very long. Her shoulders, which were bare (and he assumed she was nude beneath the sheet), were round and had some muscle on them. She had pale, unblemished skin, and although her face was lost in the depression of the pillow, he could see soft, full lips. She reminded him of a French actress, the kind you don't think too much of at the first of the film but fall in love with at the end. In any case, he had never known anyone like that, certainly no one who would end up in his bed.

A lot of stories begin like this, he thought. You wake up and the world has changed and you don't know what you should do and you realize that panic is the most basic form of existence. And so you start to panic and you think of all the people in your life who can make things right. Shelby knew no one who could make things right, so, with hesitation, he spoke to her. Hey, he said. He kicked the bed a little and regretted it the moment he did it. What kind of brute was he? She certainly looked harmless enough, and a lovely woman in your bed, no matter how she got there, that's a blessing. There are reasons you've gone so many years without making love, Shelby, he thought, and kicking a woman out of your bed is symptomatic of that problem. Your panic is your problem, not hers, so you don't need to spread it around, because it's a lot like fire.

He scratched his head. He moved his palm over his morning stubble. He looked out the window: it was sunny, perhaps windy. He looked to the bed. He stretched. He yawned, but it was a fake yawn, complete with a patting hand over his mouth. He wanted to kick the bed again because at least something would happen. Just try to remember, he thought. What did you do last night? I went to bed, alone. Did the bed jostle during the night? No, it didn't budge. He tried to recall his dreams, but he couldn't recall any dreams. So what?

He left the bedroom and shut the door behind him. That wasn't what he wanted to do, but was what he had to do. What he had to do was call the police, maybe call the institutions, wasn't there one not far from here? Get your coat and go, but it was Sunday, would they be open? Of course they'd open, an institution isn't a hardware store. I've got a woman in my bed and I don't know what do to with her, please help. Sure, they'd lock him up and he would deserve it. The phone rang. He leaped for the phone and whispered hello and someone asked for Arnold and he wondered, for a moment, if that was her name, which would mean she was a man, so he hung up the phone and when it rang again he disconnected it. He thought for a moment, pressing his temples. No, she was female, there was no doubt about that. But had the phone woken her? He put his ear to the door, listened, heard nothing, so probably she was sleeping, though perhaps she was standing, listening at the door, too. Who would move first? You're an idiot, Shelby, just go in there, wake her, wrap a sheet around her and send her on her way. Problem solved!

His stomach rumbled. In the kitchen his hands shook as he spread peanut butter on toast. Was she a cousin, or a niece? A long-lost sister? In his bed? Was she a prostitute who'd gotten the wrong address? But wouldn't she have woken him? Was this his apartment? Was this a practical joke? She's lost, she's lost, he thought; that was the only thing that made sense. She's lost and she's hungry and if you throw her to the street, that'll be the end of her. Sure, and then her lovely, heart-shaped face will be all over the news and everyone will feel the tragic loss, and next to her face will be your thin face, Shelby, your cruel eyes and rigid mouth. She will be the forlorn angel and you the man who never smiled. Rocks will be thrown through your windows, notes calling you a murderer will slip under your door. She's lost, he thought, and she needs help. Or maybe she thought you looked kind, Shelby. Maybe she followed you home. Crawled up a brick wall three stories and entered the bedroom window.

Or maybe she loved him? Maybe she had always loved him and he had never noticed. Maybe she had watched him stroll up and down the streets, newspaper under his arm, that bounce in his step and generous smile he had for all whom he encountered. She worked in the back of the newsstand, too shy to come forth and say hello, scribbled hearts and arrows on a pink notepad. And why was that any more unreasonable than her being a lost prostitute? He lay on couch and watched the bedroom door.

Quickly he drifted off, but falling into sleep was like sinking below water, and the bubbled panic jerked him awake. It's just a woman, he reminded himself. It's not a bear, though this is unbearable. Rest for a moment then pick up the phone and call someone, anyone. He could call his mother, on the other side of the country, but he'd have to yell, as deaf as she was. He could call his ex wife, but didn't want to, hadn't spoken to her in a year, and surely there'd be children screaming. Whaddaya want me to do 'bout it, huh? Cripes. Or the police…

He sat up when he thought he heard a noise from the bedroom. But no, it was only a lock across the hallway. He half expected her to come screaming, holding the sheet over her body, crying, pointing. Good God, this could go badly. But wait, he thought, I'd was beside her, moving, snoring. I rolled out of bed and stretched and moaned and then I saw her, there, alive, breathing. Sleeping. Surely she'd woken during the night and saw me. Shelby sat up: how the hell do you end up in someone's else's bed and not know it? The only thing more intimate would have been some stranger suddenly pulling the shower curtain aside, stepping in and soaping your back.

The police would laugh. Do you want us to shoot her?

Not an hour had passed since he'd woken. The clock on the kitchen counter ticked loudly, was the only sound coming from the apartment, and he thought of sneaking it into the bedroom, putting it on pillow next to her head, and then? Running? Leaving the door open and hiding down the hallway? Maybe she'll just wander out? Hell, maybe she's not even there. The policemen, brows furrowed, enter the bedroom and say buddy, look, we've got better things to do…

He decided to make coffee. Coffee would help him think, yes. Coffee, that's what you do in the morning, you make coffee, it percolates, there's aroma, and there she would be, rubbing her eyes, saying hi, I guess you made coffee, smells good. Right, and you'd sit at the table and she'd explain it all, and oh, right, and you'd laugh, exclaim I never thought of that! He paced while it brewed. The coffee would only make him more nervous. He held back the urge to shout. Shelby, he told himself, you need to do something about this. But she can't sleep forever, so why not just sit here, drink coffee, and wait?

But that would drive him crazy.

The coffee wasn't very good, and he realized he'd not paid attention while making it. Should he make another pot? Yes, he shut off the machine, emptied the carafe, cleaned the filter, decided to use fresh beans, ground them, checked the door behind him, measured carefully this time and sighed hoping she'd hear all this tapping and whirring and snapping and gurgling. Maybe she did, maybe she was backed against the wall, eyes searching the room for a route of escape. God, maybe she'd jump out the window, break both legs, point up in agony and what would everyone think? I swear I didn't know her, had never seen her before. Maybe you pushed her, the detective will say. Shit. I honestly had never seen her before in my life. Not until she was in your bed this morning? Yes, exactly. Go knock on the door, Shelby, say look, I don't know who you are, or why you are in my bed, but I think you should leave. If you are in trouble and need help, let's talk about it.

It was a simple solution. What'd become of him that he couldn't face a challenge head on? Loss of job, dwindling severance. Then divorce, followed by two years of impotence. An utter lack of sex drive, his psychologist noted. You may possibly feel emasculated. Try growing a beard, or visiting local parks in summer. Stroll around and watch the young girls frolic. It will do you a world of good. And why hadn't he asked advice upon finding a naked woman in your bed? Why, make love to her! Play the role of the man, Shelby, it's all any woman wants. She won't leave until you make love to her. Dammit. He heard the judge asking why in the world he'd choose rape over a knock on the door, a shaking of a shoulder? You seem a reasonable man, you won't survive a week in prison.

Shelby sipped the coffee, added some cream, concluded he'd got it just about right this time, and before he could stop himself he was walking toward the bedroom door, the coffee cup in hand, slowly turning the doorknob, heart pounding, opening the door a crack, peeking through and.... He closed the door and went back to the kitchen counter.

He hadn't been able to make out all of the bed, but the sheet was off and unless she was curled in the far lower corner of the bed, she was no longer in the bed. Ah, damn, and he'd spilled coffee on his pajamas and on the floor. He set about wiping it up.

Was she hiding behind the door? In the closet? Standing at the window? All he'd wanted to do was give her the coffee and look her in the eye. It would have went from there. But now she was no longer in bed! Shelby began to laugh. It was an awkward laugh, one that belonged to a poor actor, the kind who are limited to local dinner theatres, but it was a genuine laugh, though he had no idea why he was laughing. If anything, this was when he should have been utterly silent, listening for a clue – she would have heard him, seen him open the door, and now she was...

Listening to him laugh.

He covered his mouth and hid in the washroom, but the moment he was in the washroom he knew it'd been the wrong decision. Bad move, Shelby, he said while pacing the narrow space. At least the laughing had stopped. And Shelby, though he loved the smell of coffee, couldn't stand the smell of it on his clothing, so he removed his pajamas and threw them in the hamper thinking he had a clean bathrobe in the washroom closet but no, it was in the bedroom, still in the laundry bag from Friday, so now he'd be wearing nothing but a towel when he confronted her. Great. Or he could rush into the bedroom, grab some clothes, rush out, get dressed, collect himself, prepare a speech, and then return to the bedroom acting as if he hadn't just rushed in there like a fool. I am going to go insane. I am going to die in my bathroom, hugging the toilet, talking to the toilet brush. Meanwhile, you're still naked Shelby.

There were noises in the kitchen.

Of course there were noises in the kitchen, of course she was out there now, looking for something to eat, or money. Maybe she'd phone friends. They'd rob him blind, leave nothing but the toaster. Shelby got to his knees and cleaned out the stuffed-up keyhole, the old toilet paper now yellow and brittle. He could hear her but not see her, and then ah ha, there she was, passing quickly a blur but still nude. She was checking cupboard doors, then what sounded like the broom closet door, then the fridge, then coming his way. Hips and the dark dot of a navel and a thatch of black pubic hair and Shelby stood and held the doorknob and snapped the lock's hook into the jutting loop. She was turning the doorknob. What should he say? She sighed. He wanted to say: you're alive? So what, did he think she was ghost?

She knocked. Shelby was speechless, felt like he was five years old hiding from his father, not that he'd done anything wrong but sometimes guilt is assumed and the purpose of the mysterious is to seek retribution. Get a hold of yourself, Shelby, this is a harmless naked female knocking at your bathroom door, this is about as harmless a situation as one could possibly imagine, she is the one in danger. Yet why is she fearless? There's no one else in the apartment, this isn't a trap, you fool. Damn it. Shelby undid the lock and opened the door without pause and he would raise his arms, say what the hell is going on here, this is my apartment, what do you want, and where was she? The kitchen was empty. The bedroom door was open and the sheets were on the floor. He checked the broom closet, he checked behind the sofa, checked the bedroom again and dammit, dug out his bathrobe from the laundry bag, wrapped it around him, tied it snugly, went back into the kitchen saw the note on the counter, next to the coffee mug.

There was only one word on the note, which was written on an ear of cardboard ripped from the coffee filter box, but Shelby spent a lot of time considering the word, though it could only be interpreted in one way, that she would return, for the note said, simply, "Tomorrow?"

*Untitled # 3, Roméo Savoie, 2012*

# About the Contributors

**Elaine Amyot** studied art at the Université de Moncton and has had many solo and group exhibitions in the Maritime provinces and has also been exhibited in France. She is a founding member of Galerie Sans Nom and of Galerie 12, in Moncton. In 1990 she received the medal of the city of Moncton for exceptional services rendered to the community. Her life as an artist was shown on the program *Trajectoire* (SRC.RDI) in November, 1996. In the summer of the year 2000 she coordinated *Présence 27*, an exhibition-installation of women artists at the Galerie d'Art de l'Université de Moncton. In 2010 she published her first book, *The Seven Gates: A Memoir of a Descent.*

**Zev Bagel** (the pen-name for Warren Redman) is a prolific author of non-fiction. He also has three as yet unpublished novels waiting for the right publisher. His latest is *The Last Jew in Hania,* set in Crete and (among other places) Moncton and Shediac.

**Elizabeth Blanchard's** short stories have appeared in a number of literary journals including *Lichen Arts & Letters Preview, Windsor Review, Room of One's Own* and *Dalhousie Review*, and anthologized in *Hard Ol' Spot: an Anthology of Atlantic Canadian Fiction* and in *Mothering Canada:Interdisciplinary Voices* by Demeter Press. She won the Writers' Federation of New Brunswick Literary Competition, and is a recipient of a Creation Grant by the New Brunswick Arts Board. She lives in Dieppe, New Brunswick.

**Noeline Bridge** writes non-fiction and attempts to write novels. Her non-fiction has thrice won first prize in the Writers' Federation of New Brunswick literary competitions. For money and more instant gratification, she indexes books. Her articles on indexing have appeared in professional journals and as book chapters; her book, *Indexing Names*, was published in 2012. She also co-authored *Royals of England: A Guide for Readers, Travelers, and Genealogists*, which was published in 2005.

**Edward Lemond** grew up in Indiana and California and came to Canada in 1969. After 24 years in Halifax he moved to Moncton, New Brunswick. He has published several poems in *The Antigonish Review* and short stories in various Canadian literary journals. One of his poems was chosen for the anthology, *Crossing Lines: Poets Who Came to Canada in the Vietnam War Era,* from Seraphim Editions. His novel, *September 11, Blow Soft,* appeared in 2012. He was a principal organizer for the annual Frye Festival in Moncton, from 2000 through 2011.

**Beth McLaughlin** was born in Grand Falls, New Brunswick, and currently lives in Moncton. She has been dabbling in writing – short stories, articles, and plays – for a few decades. She's a retired teacher.

**Roméo Savoie** was born in Moncton and holds a Master's in Fine Arts from l'Université du Québec à Montréal, a Bachelor's degree in architecture from l'École des Beaux-Arts de Montréal, and a B.A from l'Université de Moncton. From 1959 to 1970 he worked as an architect, before turning to painting in the late 60s. Essentially an action painter, Savoie transmits his great energy to his artwork, using themes he has also elaborated in his literary work. He has had numerous solo and group shows, and he has won many awards and prizes, including the Miller Brittain Excellence Award and the Strathbutler award. He also won the Eloize prize for visual artist of the year, 1998. His literary work includes six collections of poetry. He is a member of the Order of Canada.

**Nancy King Schofield** (Saint John, N.B.) began her artistic career in music. She graduated from St. Joseph's Hospital in 1961 and received a BFA from Mount Allison University in 1991. Schofield helped found Galerie 12 at the Aberdeen Cultural Center where she rented an artist studio for nine years. She began a writers' group in 1999, the Breach House Gang, that currently numbers ten members. She celebrated Northrop Frye's 100th Birthday (Ellipse, no. 87-88, 2012) with poetry and helped launch *The Breach House Anthology* (2010). Her text is often used to add surface interest in her art. She has presented over one hundred exhibitions since 1991 and is part of many collections. In 2010 she received first prize in poetry from the WFNB.

**David Skyrie** is a writer and visual artist residing in Grand Barachois, New Brunswick. He has a degree in Arts from Concordia University in Montreal. He started painting in 2000, after a one-year stay in Brazil, and works in a variety of media. Dave's current work is an exploration of abstract forms and textures on larger canvas. A member of the

AAAPNB (Assoc. of Acadian Artists of N.B.) and the Writers Federation of New Brunswick, Dave has also published two books of poetry. His work appears presently in both private and public collections in Canada. His studio/gallery is located in Shediac, N.B. and is open to the public.

**Lee D. Thompson** was born and raised in Moncton, New Brunswick. His short fiction has appeared in literary journals across Canada and the US, and in the anthologies *Victory Meat: New Fiction from Atlantic Canada*, *The Vagrant Revue of New Fiction*, *Hard Ol' Spot: An Anthology of Atlantic Canadian Fiction*, and *New Brunswick Short Stories*. His book *S. a novel in [xxx] dreams* was published by Broken Jaw Press in 2007. He is the editor of the fiction journal *Galleon* and has twice been awarded Creation Grants from ARTSNB, as well as a Creation Grant from the Canada Council for the Arts. He is currently executive director of the Writers' Federation of New Brunswick, and he is the new Atlantic Canada rep for the Writers Union of Canada.

# Acknowledgements / Credits

**Noeline Bridge:** "Pentecostalist Wedding" and "Night Bus to Amsterdam" won first prizes in the Writer's Federation of New Brunswick annual literary competitions.

**Lee D. Thompson:** "Hairball Man" was first published in *Riddle Fence 2*.

www.ingramcontent.com/pod-product-compliance
Lightning Source LLC
Chambersburg PA
CBHW031429250626
47155CB00004B/1676